Sparx

Issue 4

Anthology of Writing by the

Society of Women Writers Victoria

First published by Pinion Press, an imprint of Busybird Publishing 2019

ISBN 978-1-925949-54-4

Authors: Various

Cover image: Paula Wilson

Layout: Busybird Publishing

Editing Committee: Errol Broome, Caroline Webber, Mary Jones, Rebecca Maxwell, Lynne Santos, Paula Wilson.

Typeset in Palatino 12pt

This anthology is a production of the Society of Women Writers Victoria. The Society is a network linking professional and novice women authors, poets, journalists and general writers across Australia.

www.swwvic.org.au

Contents

Introduction

Welcome to the fourth issue of *Sparx*. You are invited to come on a journey with the members of the Society of Women Writers through their poetry, fiction and nonfiction.

This issue includes the four prize-winning poems from the 2019 Kathryn Purnell Poetry Prize as judged by Janette Fernando.

I would like to dedicate this issue of *Sparx* to the late Dulcie Stone who, through her generous donations, contribution of stories, and work on the editing committee, has been instrumental in the continued success of the anthology.

Now sit back in your favourite chair and enjoy the tales these writers are sharing with you.

Paula Wilson
President

The Carousel Ponies

Margaret Amery White

The iron gates are opening, and a new day at the carnival is about to commence.

Children are running through the gateway and excitedly calling to each other. The sound of anxious parents trying to keep up with their children is almost drowned by the tinkling music box inside the carousel.

The carousel is a favourite with young children, and a race to jump on to the best pony is the cause of much merriment.

Silver, the biggest and most magnificent pony, stands on the outside circle of the carousel. Although his silver coat has worn thin, his pink tail and mane ragged and flimsy, the gold studs on his saddle tarnished, the children see his beautiful smile.

Velvet, the smallest pony, has been on the carousel hidden behind the chariot. Her black coat is still shiny, and her mane and tail thick and lush. She wears a red saddle but this is not enough to make her smile.

Each day, when Velvet watches the children climb on the big pony's back, her head droops lower behind the chariot until she almost disappears from sight.

There is something mysterious and magical about the carousel ponies – known only to children. Every night, when all the carnival people are asleep the ponies talk to each other.

One night, Silver heard sobbing from behind the chariot.

'Why are you crying, little black pony?'

'It isn't fair,' grumbled Velvet. 'Every day the children rush to ride on your scruffy saddle. Look at me. I'm beautiful, and you're so shabby.'

Silver shook his head. 'They don't see how shabby I've become. They see my smile. Do you know that a smile is infectious?'

'What do you mean, infectious?'

'It means it is something you can catch.'

'Why would I want to catch your silly old smile?'

'That's sad,' said Silver. 'If you hold your head high and catch my smile, the children will see it and come and ride on your beautiful red saddle.'

Velvet tilted her head. 'Do you really believe that if I catch your smile the children will want to ride on me?'

'I do,' replied Silver. 'I'll smile at you tomorrow. When you catch my smile, lift your head up high and I promise the children will come to you.'

Next morning, Velvet did as the big pony told her. And she became infected with Silver's smile.

The first ride came. The second. The third. The children still raced to ride on Silver. They never noticed the little black pony, struggling to keep her wooden head above the chariot, and trying to hold back the tears from her big glass eyes.

The sun began to fade behind the carnival tents and Velvet felt her head sinking. She knew that there would only be a few more rides before the carnival closed for the day. She stretched her head and watched a little girl about to climb on Silver's back. Then her mother shook her index finger and called, 'Jemima, only one more ride.'

Velvet lifted her head higher and smiled directly at the little girl. Jemima caught her smile. She turned and walked behind the chariot and climbed on Velvet's back as the music started and the carousel began to turn.

The carousel gathered speed. Jemima clutched Velvet's thick black mane and dug her heels into her side. It hurt but Velvet didn't mind. For the first time she was proud to be a carousel pony.

When the carnival closed for the day and all the carnival people were asleep, Velvet told Silver how wonderful she felt when the little girl tugged at her mane.

Silver noticed that Velvet's mane looked a little wispy and her saddle showed signs of wear.

The big pony decided it was time to tell Velvet the carousel ponies' secret.

'Velvet, you have seen how worn and scruffy I've become, and how happy I am when the children pull my mane and rub the shine from my silver coat.'

'Yes,' replied Velvet, 'but why do you smile when you grow shabbier every day?'

'If you listen carefully to me, I will tell you a secret.'

'I don't know what to do with a secret.'

'It's simple. All you have to do is keep it to yourself and it will be our secret.'

'That will be easy because you're the only one who listens to me.'

'The shabbier I become, the happier I am, because when the carnival closes at the end of summer, workmen come and take all the shabby and worn out ponies. They drive them on their truck and dump them in a lush green paddock.'

'That's terrible,' cried Velvet. 'What if this happens to you?'

'I hope it does. Don't look so worried. The truck tips them into a paddock where all the most loved ponies spend the rest of their lives. They graze and play among shady trees. I've watched many of my friends leave with the workmen, and this year I hope I'm shabby enough to be selected. Maybe if you keep smiling you will be chosen to come with me.'

'I don't want to be put in a truck and left in a strange place.'

'Don't worry, little friend, I'll watch over you. Time to go to sleep. The carnival people will be awake soon, so we will talk again tomorrow night.'

Velvet was tired but she could not sleep. She was confused, and aware of unfamiliar emotions. She was afraid of losing her beautiful coat and lush mane, but proud that Silver had called her his friend.

She tried to imagine what it would be like to feel soft grass under her hooves instead of being attached to a wooden floor. What would it be like to feel gentle rain and the warmth of the sun, instead of a wooden roof overhead? And to hear the birds singing instead of the music box playing the same jingling tune, sunrise to sunset. And what if she could swish her tail and toss her mane out of her glass eyes? How would that feel?

Next morning promised a sunny day so it was expected that many children would visit the carnival. The carousel music box began to wind up, and the shrieks of children as they raced to jump on the ponies caused Velvet's little wooden heart to beat faster.

She stretched her head up and smiled at Silver. Strange! She was sure she felt a twinkle in her glass eyes.

Velvet twitched her rubber ears and heard the familiar voice of Jemima. This time the little girl brought her cousin, Katie.

Jemima approached the smallest pony and called, 'Katie, come and see my friend, Velvet.'

While Jemima climbed on Velvet's back, Katie stroked the side of her head.

'She has beautiful eyes, Jemima. I'm sure she is smiling at me.'

The carousel stopped. It was Katie's turn to ride on Velvet. By the end of the day, many children had sat on Velvet's red saddle and clung to her shabby mane. When night fell she was tired, but happy.

Days passed, Velvet became popular, and grew shabbier. Her saddle became tattered, and the silver studs lost their sparkle.

The next evening, when the carousel stopped after the last ride, and the carnival folk had gone to their tents, Silver said to Velvet, 'I think you are even shabbier than me.'

Velvet felt her mane was shabby but it didn't make her sad.

The final day of the carnival season dawned bright and sunny. Excited children raced to ride on Velvet's red saddle.

At the end of the day, Silver called to Velvet. 'Tomorrow morning the men will come in a truck to collect the most loved, worn-out ponies.'

Unfamiliar sensations kept Velvet awake. She felt her tattered tail and mane. Her once beautiful saddle was cracked and faded, its gold fringe in tatters.

The next morning, the friends watched two men climb out of a truck, each carrying a box of tools. They jumped on to the carousel and approached Silver.

Velvet watched the men unbolt Silver and toss him into the back of the truck. She gasped at the sight of her friend being treated so roughly.

Looking around, the truck driver called, 'Don't believe there are any others ready to dump. Jump in Joe, and we'll be off.'

The truck finally disappeared through the carnival gateway.

Velvet was afraid she would never see Silver again. Her little wooden heart beat so loudly that she didn't hear the truck return.

'You must have left your toolbox on the carousel,' yelled the driver to Joe.

As Joe jumped on the carousel, a gust of wind blew, causing it to turn. He looked up and noticed Velvet's shabby mane.

'My, you're a sorry sight, little black pony,' he said.

He called to the driver, 'Help me remove this little shabby one.'

The driver climbed down from his truck.

'Well, I never,' he said, scratching his head. 'This was the sad little black pony I thought would last for ages. I put the bright red saddle on her back to make her look more cheerful. I never noticed her sweet smile before.'

He removed the tools from his box and eased Velvet from the floor. The two men carried her to the truck and tossed her beside Silver. Velvet smiled at her friend. Silver was so relieved to see the little pony that tears spilled down his wooden cheeks.

The truck drove along the road, past rolling green paddocks where ponies grazed happily and cantered under shady trees.

Suddenly, the truck swerved without any warning, just missing a kangaroo that jumped across the road. Velvet rolled against Silver. She felt her little wooden heart pounding. Nothing like this had ever happened before. She was afraid.

Without warning, the back of the truck began to lower, and the two ponies slid out into a lush green paddock.

The driver turned to Joe, and said, 'That's it for the day. We can now go home.'

Early one morning, two little girls riding bikes saw ponies galloping happily across the paddocks under shady trees.

'Look, Jemima,' called Katie, as she watched a small black pony and a beautiful big white pony turn and gallop towards them. 'They look like the two ponies from the carnival carousel.'

'They do!' replied Jemima. 'I can see shiny pearls spilling down the white pony's cheek, and the sweet smile on little black one. I think she is smiling at us.'

'I know she is,' said Katie.

Jemima and Katie rode home knowing they shared a secret with the carousel ponies.

Listen

Janice Williams

First place in the Kathryn Purnell Poetry Prize, 2019

Listen
listen to the silent bush
silent?
listen closer yet, and hear
the opera of early dawn

Night-owl boobook
yawns and performs
a weary two-note plainchant
bows and retires
for livelier choirs

Trickly, chuckly, creekly noises
there's been rain, the bush rejoices

Fleetly tripping, flitting, skipping
sprightly tiny chorus patter
scrub wren, wagtail, robins chatter
trill a lively intermezzo
Hey, presto!

Please
hear the bees
in hollowed-out trees
vibrate, resonate
no solo act these

Glockenspiel frog-bells all clink, chime and glonk
oboe of woodwind-ducks burble and honk

Kookaburra, martial bird
strident, mocking threat and malice
spills his vibrant laughter-chalice
climbing riotous crescendo
inviting lesser birds to join
a counterpoint diminuendo

Winds in the eucalypts whisper and sing
harp strings of sheoak chords ripple and zing

Carolling magpies chortle and trill
in lyric soprano, their harmonies, glees
euphonic arpeggios, roundels and airs
pouring fortissimo, songs to the trees

Lighting the scenery, summer sun wakes
a chitter of flycatchers, warning of snakes

Listen
as nature rejoices with bush chorale voices
madrigal, glee, serenade, air and scherzo
descant, roulade, divine obbligato
calling out madly and gladly in pleasure
discordant harmony, unrehearsed measure

And it's said the bush is silent

Omi

Margrit Zalisz

When I think of my childhood, I think of Omi. She was there when I took that first step across the threshold from the unconscious to the conscious. That indelible moment, the first to stamp itself into the book of my memories.

We were alone at home when the telephone rang to awaken us from sleep and simultaneously tear me from the haze of my infant days. I sat upright in bed while Omi hastened to the telephone. When she came back, she informed me: 'Little Monika has been born.'

On the following day, we went to visit my mother and baby sister in hospital, while our father was stationed somewhere at the French front.

The political events prior to World War II had rendered it necessary that my grandmother move into our household, and thus my sister and I walked close by Omi's side through our childhood, through our teenage and young adult days.

While my sister was still a baby, Omi belonged exclusively to me. She travelled with me to the sea-side and it must have been then, at this first encounter with the ocean, that my great love for the billowing waves was aroused. We bathed, romped about in the dunes and collected shells in order to decorate the rampart we had erected around our beach chair. I was allowed to ride along the beach promenade in a pony-drawn coach and sit well-behaved next to Omi to listen to my first Promenade Concert.

Omi took me on a visit to her friends in the country. She introduced me to the big watch dog, put a newly born lamb and baby rabbits into my arms. She placed the first silky chick into my hand and treated my knees, chafed after tumbling out of the apple tree.

With Omi, I went shopping. With Omi, I took my baby sister for a stroll and Omi was the one who tied the large ribbon into my hair and took me along to her ladies' coffee-parties.

In the height of summer we would leave the city with Omi for our weekend cottage. She roamed with us through forest and heather, watched my first swimming attempts, held onto my skirt when I bent too far out from our boat to pick water-lilies, and dried our tears when a bee or wasp stung us. In the evening she would scrub us in the big wash tub behind the huge red-currant hedge before popping us into bed.

To Omi we took both our large and small worries. To her we took our broken doll. With Omi we visited our first pantomime. When the snow fell, she would produce our sleigh and pull us through the white splendour. Eagerly, we would help her as she baked gingerbread; and when, in the evening, the apples sizzled as they baked in the recess of the tiled stove, she would read to us, tell us fairy tales and sing with us the first carols of Christmas.

Then, one day, Omi was gone.

'Where is Omi?' I asked my parents.

'She's on holidays.'

I couldn't remember my grandmother ever having been away from us for such a number of days.

'It's about time she came home,' I sulked, deciding to go and help in our salon. Brush and comb in one pocket of my little white uniform, and the change the customers had given me as tips jingling in the other to assure everyone of my riches, I climbed up on my foot stool to comb the ladies' freshly shampooed hair and passed curlers to the adult attending the customer.

'Where is Omi?' The customers also wanted to know, and received the same answer. Only many years later did I learn of Omi's whereabouts at that particular time.

Those were the dark years. The war was raging and Germany played its unfortunate role allotted by history and fate.

My father had returned from France. He had been dismissed as being unworthy to fight in the German army when, after being called upon to divorce my mother, due to her being of fifty percent Jewish descent, he declined to do so. Thereupon he had reopened his hairdressing salon, telling the Guild that his dismissal was due to ill health.

The business flourished. On the outside all seemed well. The Hitler portrait hung in the display window and customers who shouted 'Heil Hitler' were greeted with the same, while all along my parents and Omi shuddered each time the doorbell rang, in terrible fear of the Gestapo.

I remember little of those times except that I was a happy child and so was my sister. I enjoyed helping in the salon or, if the fancy took me, being a customer. I would put on my hat and coat, clutch my handbag under my arm and, leaving through the door of our apartment, enter through the salon. The apprentices would, when free, give me a shampoo, a marcel-wave or manicure, and found me probably quite useful as a model. But all the time, the centre of our childhood was Omi.

Life was good – apart, maybe, from the annoying fact of being dragged into the air-raid shelter in the middle of many a night – and all I record here of Omi's and my parents' anxiety is what I learned much later.

There was, for instance, the incident when Omi's friend took my sister in her pram, and myself by the hand, for a walk in the park, and a neighbour remarked: 'Fancy you taking those little bastards for a walk!' while spitting onto the ground in order to strengthen her remark. The blissful ignorance of our young age did not, of course, allow this cutting insult to penetrate, but Omi's friend was certainly taken aback. Luckily, though, she stood by Omi's side, as most of her friends did, and the slanderous lady did nothing more to harm my family. But then came the day my father did not guard his tongue.

A customer, who lived in the same apartment house as we did, our salon being at the right of it and a greengrocer shop to the left, came to my father in great agitation. Since the salon was empty, he confided in him that his wife was Jewish and that he was consumed by worry. Thinking that the knowledge of someone else in a similar plight would comfort the man, my father told him of Omi's Jewish descent. She, too, even though she had taken the Christian faith upon marrying my grandfather, was in the same great danger as the man's wife of being transported to one of the concentration camps, and that it was getting increasingly hard to conceal the fact of her lineage.

Poor Omi. Why did this man have to repeat all he was told to his wife, and why did his foolish wife have to speak about it to the janitor? Several days later the Gestapo did call. Luckily it was not a trip to the concentration camp for Omi, but a sentence for an eight week prison term for not holding a Jewish identification card and not adopting the additional name of Sarah as decreed in 1938.

So this had been Omi's 'holiday' when I missed her so badly. What must have been Omi's thoughts behind the bars of one of Berlin's Women's Prisons? Omi, who could not hurt a fly. I had never heard her mention it, and my desire to know more about her life, and my wish that she had kept a diary of her colourful existence, came too late.

Had Omi thought about her childhood days, embittered by a stepmother who prompted her and her sisters to leave home at a tender age? Young and vulnerable, they had to fend for themselves, alone in a big city without a profession, looking for work after having lived in a well-to-do home. Or had she thought about her husband, and his love and care after those difficult years? About when he took her and their young children to Russia as his occupation required? She must have liked it there, for she told us anecdotes from those happy but brief days, to which the First World War had put an abrupt end. Grandfather was interned and Omi and the children were laboriously transported back to Germany. After the war, when the family was reunited, her husband was a broken man. Sick in heart and soul from the hardships endured in Siberia, he died soon afterwards. Did Omi think about the years in which she had to bring up her children by herself, and of the cleaning job she took to maintain them? As both her son and daughter grew up, life was beginning to show its brighter side once more. But happiness was to be no lasting thing. Soon, Hitler came onto the scene.

With Omi imprisoned, my father did everything in his power to get her freed. He told the authorities that it was he who told Omi not to get a Jewish passport. He bribed, he implored, and then he enticed one of his brothers, a member of the Nazi Party, to help. It worked. Omi's term was reduced to four weeks. But the Gestapo kept an eye on her, paying regular visits to our home, waiting for the moment they could include Omi in one of their transportations to a concentration camp. During that time, her sister was taken to Theresienstadt, then her brother and his wife, none of them to return.

When in 1943 our salon and flat were partly damaged in an air-raid, my father took the opportunity to take Omi to the country, to the village where my mother, sister and I had been evacuated shortly before. This was Omi's salvation, because on his return my father was drafted into a prison division of the Organisation Todt, a battalion where his comrades were Half-Jews, Negroes, Gypsies and other undesirables. Cheap fodder for dangerous missions such as bomb disposals.

In the country, Omi was relatively safe due to the decency of the Mayor, a distant relative of my father's. Thus, Omi survived the Nazi Regime and the war, as did the rest of my immediate family.

While Berlin tried to rise from ruins and ashes, and the first care parcels were received to delight hungry stomachs, a letter from Omi's Jewish nephew arrived from Australia, asking whether we would like to join him and his brother in their new homeland. Omi and my parents decided it would be a good idea, and after a number of months in a displaced persons camp in the Allgaeu, the *Surriento* brought us to Melbourne.

In no time, Omi had endeared herself to the children of our neighbourhood. The baker, the milkman, all were her friends. Omi, who seemed to become smaller as I gained height, now merely reached up to my armpits. Always busy, hardly ever to be seen without her cotton apron, she looked after the household and planted flowers in the garden while my sister went to school and my parents and I to work. At the evening courses, Omi once more took her place on the school bench in order to learn English.

When the young immigrants from Germany flocked to Melbourne, they found, like each little stray cat, love and warmth in Omi's presence and our home represented a bit of homeland to many.

Omi saw to our dowry. According to tradition, my sister and I had to stitch our initials into each piece of linen she purchased for us. Pieces I still have. Pieces which constantly remind me of our dearly-loved little Omi. Omi – who baked, cooked, knitted, embroidered; who cared for and was there for so many. And many there were who cried with us, when all too suddenly Omi departed from our lives.

A Pachyderm at Peak Hour

Leigh Hay

It's not yet 5pm and
Fitzsimons Lane is a car park.
Clearly I'm in for the long sit –
if only my car had wings.

I sigh, lift heavy eyes
and stare
into the shimmering blue
of a summer sky …

and then I see it!

an albino elephant charging
trunk lifted in full bellow
tail a streaking contrail
ears puffed and wildly flapping
a smug smile forming just under its eye.

I am captivated.

An albino elephant, what a sight!
I will recount this revelation
to my three year old granddaughter
who relishes talk of such things.

Meanwhile, someone is tooting.
The traffic has moved a metre.

Jessica's Driving Lesson

Nanice Leggas

Mrs Fenshaw jabbed her finger at the open street directory. 'There! I knew I'd seen a road like that in our area! It runs through undeveloped land, no houses and no junctions, perfect for your driving lesson, Jessie.'

'At this time of night?' Mr Fenshaw asked, without taking his eyes off the TV.

'Why not?' asked Jessica. 'Less traffic. And I have to learn to drive at night, anyway.'

'Yeah! Come on, Mum. Let's go for a spin!' called Luke, who was feeling bored.

'Be careful!' Mr Fenshaw called as his family disappeared out of the door.

Jessica couldn't drive well enough to tackle local streets with all their traffic, so Mrs Fenshaw drove when they set out in her small battered sedan. Mr Fenshaw wouldn't allow his daughter to learn to drive in his nice new Ford.

'Do you reckon we'll make it?' Luke worried when the car chugged at the first corner and threatened to stall.

'Of course. The car's just cold.' His mother grated the gear shift into second. 'But it would be easier if you could learn in an automatic, Jessie. There it is! Axeford Road.'

'Axeford Road!' Luke repeated. 'What a name!'

The narrow gravel road was lined on either side by dense bush. There were streetlights at the beginning, but these soon petered out.

'There, what did I tell you? Not a house or a car in sight.' Mrs Fenshaw's tone was a little less confident. She switched on the high beams. 'I wasn't expecting it to be so dark.'

'It's perfect, Mum,' said Jessica. 'Are you going to let me drive?'

Mrs Fenshaw pulled over and they swapped seats.

Luke waved his mother's phone from the back seat. 'There's no mobile phone coverage!'

'Don't play with my phone please, Luke,' his mother replied. 'Now Jessie, don't go too close to the edge. We don't want to get bogged out here in the wilderness.'

Jessica juggled the clutch and accelerator, and set off smoothly. In a few moments, she relaxed. Although there were several sharp turns, the road was mercifully straight and flat. The headlights shone on the wall of tree trunks on both sides of the road.

'Are you sure this road leads somewhere?' Luke asked.

'Yes. It comes out onto another highway, I think,' said Mrs Fenshaw.

'How soon?'

'Oh bother, I forgot the street directory.'

In the distance, a figure appeared walking along the roadside in the same direction as they were driving.

'Mum!' Jessica shrieked. 'A pedestrian! What do I do?'

'Calm down, Jessie! Just keep driving, nice and slowly.'

Jessica did as her mother instructed. They could see he was a tall, thick-set man in a lumber jacket with the hood pulled over his head. His shoulders hunched, and he was carrying an axe.

'Huh! Just as I expected!' said Luke, watching as the man receded from view. 'An axe-murderer, on Axeford Road!'

'Stop that, Luke!' Mrs Fenshaw replied. 'He's probably on his way home after felling trees.'

Jessica drew their attention to headlights ahead. 'A car's coming! Now what?'

'Take it easy,' her mother said. 'Just drive exactly as you did before. Move a bit to the left. You're doing fine. Now turn off your high beam.'

Jessica followed the instructions as a truck approached at high speed and bore down on them, hogging the road.

'Pull over!' Mrs Fenshaw yelled and reached across to grab the wheel. Jessica took her feet off the pedals, and the car stalled. The truck roared past, shaking the ground, and sending a shower of gravel behind it.

Jessica peeled her fingers from the steering wheel. 'I made a complete hash of it!'

'No, not at all.' Mrs Fenshaw spoke slowly. 'It wasn't your fault. He shouldn't have come at us like that, at such speed and without dimming his lights! Come on, start up the engine again.'

'I can't. Please, Mum. You drive home. I'm shaking!'

'Okay. But you mustn't let something like this put you off.'

Mrs Fenshaw opened the passenger door and got out. 'You know the old story. If you fall off a horse …' Her words ended in a shriek, and she disappeared. Jessica and Luke gaped at the spot where their mother should have been.

'Mum? *Mum!*'

They jumped out. The car had stalled on the edge of a steep embankment. Their mother lay at the bottom.

Jessica and Luke scrambled down, sending a mini-avalanche of loose gravel before them. Jessica checked her mother's vital signs.

'She's breathing and her pulse is working.'

'Mum, wake up!' Luke stuttered.

'Where am I? What happened?' Mrs Fenshaw croaked.

'You fell down a cliff. Are you hurt?'

'I don't think so.'

She proved it by staggering to her feet. She felt groggy and unsteady, and her head throbbed. Jessica and Luke helped her climb up to the car and into the back seat. Luke cradled her head in his lap.

'We've got to get Mum to hospital. I'll look after her. You drive.'

'Me? Drive?' Jessica gasped.

'You have to!'

Jessica approached the driver's door and noticed the precarious position they were in.

'We're too close to the edge!' She poked her head in the rear window. 'It's stable, okay, so long as you don't joggle around. But I can't drive. What if I make a mistake?'

'Then what'll we do?'

'Mum said this road meets the highway. We must be close. I'll walk,' Jessica said.

'You can't leave me here alone!'

'You'll be fine, Luke. Just lock all the doors and I'll be as quick as I can.'

'But I'm scared.'

'Don't worry, everything will be all right. Be brave for me, just this once. I've got to go.'

Jessica jogged away. She ran until a stitch in her side slowed her to a walk. She tried to ignore the forest on either side of the moonlit road.

Rounding a corner, she saw someone up ahead. He was on top of the rise, silhouetted against the starry sky. She stopped. Her heart pounded.

How could he be ahead of her now, she wondered, when they had passed him so long ago at the other end of the road? Maybe he was another man with hunched shoulders and a hooded jacket. And an axe.

As quietly as she could, she moved to the edge of the road and pressed between the bushes. She pulled up the hood of her jacket and drew the string tightly to cover all of her face, except her eyes. Thankful that her dark clothes made her virtually invisible, she waited.

He came crunching along until he was within a few paces of her. He seemed to hesitate, then continued. He passed so close that she could see the details of his clothing – enough to confirm that he was the same man they had seen earlier.

His progress around the corner gave Jessica no relief. He was heading towards Luke and her mother. She had to warn them. She crept back along the road, following the man like a cat. His strides were unnaturally long, and Jessica found herself running, darting from one clump of bushes to another.

Then the car came into view. The man had already reached it. He lifted the axe and brought it down. Jessica and Luke screamed. The front windscreen shattered but stayed in place. The man brought the axe down again. This time he made a hole in the windscreen.

Jessica shouted to draw attention from her brother.

'Jessica!' Luke screamed. 'Run!'

The figure took on a greenish glow. Jessica realised he was illuminated by the headlights of an approaching vehicle. A truck, with one headlight on high beam, was bearing down on them. The axe-man lifted his head slowly. The truck's light shone directly into the hood of his jacket.

Then, he turned and leaped over the embankment. He landed on his feet, and fled with giant strides into the forest. The truck roared past, shaking the ground, showering the car with gravel.

Jessica scrambled into the driver's seat.

'Lean back!' she yelled to Luke. 'Put your weight back as far as possible!'

The car tilted as the edge began to give way. She turned the key, which was still in the ignition. The motor spluttered and started. She shoved the car into reverse.

It shot backwards into the centre of the road. She crunched into first gear and drove off, peering through the hole in the windscreen. Second gear. Third. With her right foot planted on the accelerator, she ignored the car's protests as it ricocheted off potholes and veered around corners. A dim streetlight appeared ahead, followed by another.

'We've made it!'

As the bright lights of the highway appeared, she slowed down and stopped. Mrs Fenshaw sat up in the back seat.

'Where are we?' Before her children could reply, she added, 'You're driving well, Jessie.'

'You okay, Mum?' asked Luke.

'Not really. I've got a stinking headache. Must be a migraine coming on. Would you mind if we called it a night, Jessie? I really must go home and take something for my head.'

'I can't drive on the highway, Mum,' said Jessica.

'That's alright darling. I'll drive home from here.'

Mrs Fenshaw battled with the windscreen, then yanked it out completely.

'Look at this! I'll have to buy a new one. Some drivers have no consideration!'

Jessica and Luke were relieved to be home when their mother pulled into the driveway.

Mrs Fenshaw threw the car keys on the sideboard. 'You wouldn't believe it. A truck passed us and nearly sent us off the road. It sent up such a shower of gravel that it broke the windscreen.'

Mr Fenshaw's attention moved from the TV.

'You broke the windscreen!'

'I didn't break the windscreen! A stone from another driver flew up ...'

'And Mum fell in a ditch and hit her head,' Jessica tried to explain.

Mr Fenshaw suppressed a laugh. 'You fell in a ditch?'

'Of course I didn't fall in a ditch! I got a migraine after the windscreen broke.'

'And the axe-murderer attacked us!' Luke added.

Mrs Fenshaw looked at him sharply. 'I've had a difficult enough night as it is without you making stupid jokes!'

'But it's true!'

'He smashed the windscreen with his axe!' Jessica's words seemed hollow.

'Not you, too, Jessica,' Mrs Fenshaw groaned.

Mr Fenshaw didn't know what to make of it. 'You know, I've had a really hard day at work. Now we have to pay for a broken windscreen!'

Jessica and Luke looked at each other. Jessica made one last plea.

'Dad, we were attacked. Mum, don't you remember the axe-man? We passed him on Axeford Road, just before the truck came along?'

Mr Fenshaw peeled himself from the couch. 'You were on Axeford Road? Well, that explains everything.' He stretched and yawned. 'There was a terrible accident in that area, maybe twenty, thirty years ago. A pedestrian was killed in a hit-run accident. If I remember rightly, he was a lumberjack on his way home from work. The driver never stopped, just left him to die by the side of the road. I don't think the driver was ever caught.'

'Stop it, all of you!' shrieked Mrs Fenshaw. 'Why do you make jokes when I'm sick? I'm telling you, a stone flew up…'

'Yes, I understand,' said Mr Fenshaw. 'But the kids must have read about the accident somewhere. Do you need to see a doctor?'

'No. But I'd love a cup of tea.'

Jessica and Luke obeyed their father's signal and escaped to the kitchen.

'Why do you think the axe-man tried to kill us?' Luke whispered.

'Maybe because he can never catch the truck driver who killed him. Did you see it? He was scared of the truck. He ran away when it came back. He probably tries to kill every other driver on Axeford Road, just for revenge.'

'And only the crazy truck driver can stop him so he spends every night racing up and down Axeford Road looking for the axe-man. But that would mean the truck driver's dead, too.'

Jessica nodded, a distant look in her eyes. 'You're probably right, Luke. But no one will ever believe us.'

'And did you see his face?'

'Yes, I'll never forget it,' she replied, staring into the empty mug. 'He didn't have a face.'

Mrs Flowerdew's Journey

Caroline Webber

M rs Flowerdew awoke from a peaceful sleep, full of optimism for the new day ahead. She rolled her stiff body to the side, wriggled to the edge of the bed and let her toes search for the inside of her fluffy pink slippers, which she had conveniently set out the evening before. With a steady amount of exertion, she sat up and gave a final push out of the bed. It wasn't exactly an award-winning move, even if it did require an Olympic effort, but she was up and felt as if her legs were full of springs. There was nothing particularly striking about Mrs Flowerdew's bedroom. It was pristine and immaculately tidy, if a little tired and out of date. It was functional and feminine (pink and floral), and her feet easily followed the track made in the carpet from years of shuffling into the en-suite bathroom. Mrs Flowerdew hummed to herself, largely a tune of her own making but peppered with notes of a hymn she has sung in the Harvest Festival service at her school. She chuckled as she realised she must have learnt the hymn almost seventy-two years ago.

The water pouring from the shower head was warm and inviting and Mrs Flowerdew stepped in, and quickly lathered her body with the contents of a recently purchased bottle of Penhaligon's Wild Rose shower gel. It had been an expensive purchase, especially with the excessive import duty, but Mrs Flowerdew thought it was important to be scented with something English, and, as Penhaligon was appointed to Her Majesty Queen Elizabeth II and His Royal Highness Prince Charles, one couldn't get more English than that. Besides, she liked the name.

Internet shopping was a new hobby, which she had undertaken with a level of enthusiasm that still surprised her – and her children – since her son and daughter-in-law had bought her the latest Lenovo laptop for her birthday. She chuckled again, recalling her son's comments: 'It's not an iPad and it's not too expensive, Mum,' he reassured her. 'I didn't want to spend too much in case you didn't take to it.' *Patronising so and so*, she thought. Still, it had been her daughter-in-law's idea to attend a computer course at her local library, and what a good idea that had turned out to be.

Mrs Flowerdew stepped out of the shower and rubbed herself dry with a soft white Sheridan towel, fluffy as a dog. The week before, she had decided what to wear and her chosen outfit was folded neatly on the bedroom chair. She dressed quickly – she had intentionally chosen an outfit without tricky buttons – expertly applied her new Glossier make up, another Internet purchase, posted all the way from the US and popular among young people. *It seemed somewhat appropriate that the makeup artist for 'Fifty Shades of Grey' had included the brand in her palette*, Mrs Flowerdew thought, and ran a comb through her soft, recently styled grey hair. Before heading to the kitchen to make herself a breakfast of tea and toast with marmalade, Mrs Flowerdew gave the smart looking, shiny-black Samsonite, nestled against the bedroom wall, a reassuring pat and smiled secretly to herself; it was ready for its maiden voyage.

'Okay, please turn your devices on and we will begin,' the professional sounding voice of the class tutor bellowed from the front of the meeting room.

Amidst the general murmuring of confusion from the twelve silver surfers, gathered in the local library for the first session of *You and Your Laptop,* a couple of audible pings signalled success.

'Today we are going to start to explore the Internet. Please show your hand if you have heard the term "Google",' the highly IT-literate tutor's face visibly relaxed as he observed the full show of hands. 'Google is a popular search engine. Firstly, in order to connect with the Internet, you have to connect to the Internet,' he continued, enjoying his own joke. 'On the right-hand side of the bar running along the bottom of your screen, you will notice a small icon which looks like a fan. Click on this. A list of available networks should pop up on your screen. Click on "Library WIFI". A box will then pop up asking you to type in your password. The password is password.'

Mrs Flowerdew followed the instructions, which seemed surprisingly easy. The tutor ambled over to assist a few of her contemporaries who were adjusting their glasses and squinting at their screens, experiencing grave difficulty locating the fan.

'Once you have connected to the Internet, click on the Internet symbol. The search engine will now load and you can start exploring. The Internet contains masses and masses and masses of information. You can search for anything you like. You can read the news, you can watch live television, you can search family history records, and library records, too. You can also, ahem,' the tutor added, remembering his pitch. 'You can also find love.'

With a slightly crooked arthritic finger, Mrs Flowerdew, ignoring the tutor's poor attempt at stifling a giggle, tapped carefully on the keyboard. She was surfing.

Peter Brocklehurst: *Good evening, my dear. How are you? It looks like it is going to be a delightful day in the Cotswolds. The first beams of sunlight are warming the backs of the sheep.*

Mrs Flowerdew: *Good morning to you. I am well, thank you. How are you? Goodness, you must live out in the bush. I occasionally see sheep at the market. Oh, I hope you are not vegetarian.*

PB: *LOL. No, no. I am not vegetarian, and I too am very well, thank you.*

MF: *Excuse me, Peter, what does LOL mean?*

PB: *My goodness, apologies, my dear lady, I have been spending too much time with my grandson. I believe it means 'Laugh Out Loud.'*

MF: *Ah! LOL!*

PB: *You have changed your profile picture.*

MF: *Yes, thanks to my latest lesson!*

PB: *You are even more beautiful than I imagined.*

For the ninth time, Mrs Flowerdew leafed through the papers tucked into a notebook, and checked off a list in her head. Everything seemed to be in order. With a final glance in the hallway mirror, and a swish of her new Glossier Plum lipstick, she replaced the papers in her handbag and opened the door. In next to no time, the Uber driver was whizzing towards the airport.

At check-in, the steward complimented Mrs Flowerdew's perfume and she beamed. *I hope Mr Brocklehurst does, too.* Paperwork completed, she made her way towards the QANTAS lounge – a legacy of her late husband's numerous business trips.

A waiter helped Mrs Flowerdew to a glass of champagne and she ordered a plate of Sydney rock oysters. *What a privilege!* The pale butter-coloured Piper-Heidsieck felt cool and crisp in her mouth and the delicate bubbles gently exploded. She silently toasted: *To new beginnings and life changing adventures.*

In what seemed like next to no time, Mrs Flowerdew found herself nestled into her seat near the front of the aeroplane, being offered a blanket by the immaculately presented cabin steward. She donned her earphones and settled down to watch a movie. As luck would have it, the first on the list of choices was *Fifty Shades More*. Mrs Flowerdew quickly flicked over to the next choice – who knew what the person squashed into the seat next to her would think. Instead, she opted for *The Greatest Showman*.

'How strange,' Mrs Flowerdew murmured, standing in the arrivals hall. Being an International Visitor she had joined the back of the longest line of people she had ever set eyes on; it had taken what seemed like an eternity to pass through Customs. Mrs Flowerdew made a quick visit to the Ladies, tidied her appearance and then stood in the centre of the Arrivals Hall. And waited.

Slowly, the throng of people lessened until there were only a few remaining stragglers, like herself. From her bag, Mrs Flowerdew pulled her notebook and bundle of papers and dialled the number she had printed from one of the emails Peter Brocklehurst had sent.

Nearby, a young man, reached for the phone buzzing in his pocket.

'Hello?' he answered, cautiously.

'Mr Brocklehurst?' Mrs Flowerdew quizzed.

'Um, yes and no.'

'Yes and no?'

'Please turn around.'

Mrs Flowerdew turned and almost dropped her phone in

shock. Standing before her was an incredibly good looking man – thirty years or so younger than she had expected. Untangling her wrists from the straps of her bag, which seemed to be tied in knots worthy of a sailor, she fumbled to stow her phone away. Realising she was gawking, she was befuddled by the hundreds of thoughts racing through her head. *What on earth had she been thinking? Travelling to the other side of the world to meet a man she had met on the Internet. The Internet! Whatever would her son and daughter-in-law say?* Brushing invisible crumbs from the front of her skirt, she cleared her throat and tried to regain some degree of composure.

'Mr Brocklehurst? Peter Brocklehurst?' she stammered in the tiniest of squeaks, her heart beating loud enough, she was sure, for Mr Brocklehurst to hear.

'Yes, yes, that's me. Mrs Flowerdew?' he replied, rubbing his hand across his forehead betraying his own discomfort. 'How do you do? I am James. I am afraid I have wooed you here under false pretences.'

Pausing to steady her nerves, Mrs Flowerdew noticed a slight bead of sweat on the man's forehead. *He's as nervous as me*, she thought. The young man continued. 'I wasn't sure you would come. I, I have someone, someone very special to me, I would like you to meet. He doesn't know it yet, but I think – I know – you will like him. He would never have started chatting to someone online and so I had to take matters into my own hands. Please accept my apologies.'

'Oh,' was all Mrs Flowerdew managed to say. Realising she had been tricked and had been flirting with a man closer to her son's age than her own, she allowed herself to be led by the elbow towards a nearby airport café. Her heart skipped a beat as she was directed towards an immaculately dressed gentleman closer to her own age seated at a table, his head buried in a book. 'Oh!' she gasped. 'What lovely shiny shoes!' Realising she had spoken aloud, she turned to the young man, her cheeks flushing red and tried to recover the situation with another 'Oh!'

'Come and meet my father.'

This really was going to be life changing, thought Mrs Flowerdew, her heart fluttering.

Sonnet To My Waterbed

Trudy Oldaker

*Highly Commended for the Most Humorous Poem
in the SWWV Xmas Awards, 1989*

When all the world has left me high and dry
Rushed home at five and shut its doors on me,
I have a friend who will not pass me by,
In whose embrace I know I'll snugly be.
I say, 'Hello, my bed' and down I lie.
So soft and warm I sink into my dreams
And float back to the womb from whence I came
Before the world enticed me with its schemes
Of instant life and instant throw-away.
Dear friend, your curvy pillars will remain,
Your carvings will watch down upon my stay
As curled beneath my doona I retreat
To where all people find the time to play.
Refreshed, I rise, another rush to meet.

Ruins Of Gowar School

Judith A Green

Second place in the Kathryn Purnell Poetry Prize, 2019

a solitary hawk rides air currents
surveying motorised ants
obeying the bitumen trail
an occasional renegade detours
along a side road
creating a dust haze
left hovering
like a memory
disconnected
beside two stone walls
wire mesh protected   steel beam supported

rocks
once corralled
to a man made need
lie scattered   giant tears
shed in the dying

volcano shaped mounds
patrol the perimeter
spewing forth
incessantly moving black ant lines
emitting a pungent odour
mingling
with the tang of eucalypts

bitumen   carbon monoxide
separates
rock gatherers   builders   teachers   students
from
an occasional transient reflecting in the funereal silence

a relentless bush fly question flits
Why maintain remnants even spray can vandals ignore?

driving away
the question
travels with me

The Big Winner

Meryl Brown Tobin

An earlier version of this story was published in Writers' Friend,
2003

A wide grin on his shining moon-face beamed back at him from the newspaper's front page. The headline above a photograph of the balding man in his late sixties sent shivers of excitement racing through him even a month after the newspaper was published: *Five Million Dollar Winner*.

'Sorry, love. I have had enough,' Ernie growled into his coffee as he sat at the kitchen table, watching his wife baking. 'You'll have to tell him it's time he moved out and built himself a mansion with all his millions.'

Lucy's double chin trembled. She looked up from the pastry she was rolling and wiped her floury hands on her apron. 'I can't – he's my brother.'

Ernie glowered beneath his greying Robert Menzies' eyebrows. 'You'd never know, the way he's treated the family since he won that bloody raffle.'

'Please don't swear, Ernie.'

'Sorry. I only do it when I'm fed up.'

'I know. I'm not making excuses for Colin.' She frowned. 'I'm ashamed that he's changed – we all know he'd be nothing without you.'

'Changed!' Ernie snorted. 'Changed! One minute we've got a pet koala, who sleeps, eats and burps, then the next he's a flamin' peacock strutting about as though he owns the place.'

'Ssh! He'll hear you.'

'Hear what?' asked Colin, coming into the kitchen. 'Any chance of a cuppa?'

Ernie stood up. 'I'll leave you to it. There's a flowerbed waiting to be dug when you're through.'

Colin laughed. 'What and spoil my image? Get real, Ernie.'

Ernie turned and raised his eyebrows at Lucy. She busied herself with Colin's cup of tea. Without looking at him, she said, 'Now you've had a chance to sort yourself, I guess you'll be moving on.'

'Not on your Nellie. I know a good thing when I'm onto it. I'm not one to put on side and change my lifestyle just because I've had a bit of luck, no, sir.'

'But you don't need us now.'

'Of course I do.' He smiled. 'You're my family.'

'Yes, but …'

'No buts about it. Don't you even think I'd desert you now.'

Lucy returned to rolling her pastry.

Outside, Ernie rammed the shovel into the flowerbed and lifted up a huge weed. He shook off the earth and heaved it into the wheelbarrow. 'Where all free-loaders belong,' he muttered.

As he glared at more weeds, a car pulled into the drive. 'Hi, Dad,' called Ken. He stepped out of the car and strolled over.

'Hi, son. What have you done with Brenda and the kids?'

'Ah, you know Brenda. She reckons if Uncle Colin's going to play Scrooge, he can do it without her and the kids watching.'

'The ungrateful wretch!' said Ernie. 'Every week for years, he came home and said, "Bought me raffle ticket today. And you'll all be up there with me when I win. I'll look after you all".'

'You're right, Dad. How could we knock him when he's flashed us a $100 note? Just as well Brenda and the kids hadn't taken him seriously or they might have been looking for a trip to Disneyland.'

'The gall of the old bastard. He's had us providing him with cheap board since Ma died, shared our lives, tagged across the world with us from London, and $100 is the best he can do when he strikes it rich 30 years later.'

'If anyone's changed, it's you. You used to be so laid back and easy-going.'

Ernie pulled a face. 'Yeah, it gets to me.'

'Same here.'

Ken helped Ernie with the digging. 'Hey,' said Ernie, 'about Brenda and the kids not coming here anymore because of Colin, what about visiting your ma and me?'

'They'll be back when you give Col the flick.'

Ernie laughed. 'That's your uncle you're talking about.'

With a grin, Ken stuck his shovel upright in the ground. 'Let's go in and see Ma.'

Like someone heading for a dose of cod liver oil, Ken walked inside with his father. Colin looked up. 'Ah, me favourite nephew.' He put out his hand.

'Your only nephew.' Ken ignored Colin's outstretched hand and kissed his mother. 'Something looks good!' he said, eyeing the pie Lucy had been making.

'Hello, love,' Lucy smiled. 'Like a cuppa?'

'Thanks, Mum. I'll make it. How about I get you one?'

'That'd be nice.' The teas poured, Ken pulled out a chair and flopped down.

'So, what's it like having a rich uncle? You wouldn't believe the number of begging letters I've had since me photo appeared in the paper. They're still coming, you know.'

'And I bet you've been taking the stamps off any stamped addressed envelopes enclosed for your reply.'

'I always knew you was a man after me own heart, Ken. Keep it in the family, I say.'

Ken raised his eyebrows. 'Yeah, talking about that …' A glance at his mother's expression stopped him. He sipped his tea and said, 'So, when are you moving on, Col?'

'I'm staying put, mate. I've been telling your ma, nothing's going to change.'

'Maybe it's you who's got it wrong there.'

Lucy hurried over to Ken and pulled him to his feet. 'Ken, know you can't stay long this morning. Brenda and the kids will be waiting for you.'

Ken allowed his mother to usher him out of the room. 'Remember who loves you, Mum,' he whispered and kissed her cheek. 'Let's know when it's safe to come again.'

Lucy turned back to Colin.

'Something wrong with Ken?' he asked sucking in the flesh under his lower lip.

Lucy didn't answer.

That evening Ernie and Lucy were watching television in the living room when Colin came in and glanced at the screen. 'Not that rubbish again,' he said and made to flick the channel.

'Leave it,' said Ernie, in a cold voice.

'But …'

'Lucy likes *The Bill*, and so do I.'

Lucy nodded.

'But …'

Ernie's eyes were steely. 'If you don't like it, get your own TV. You can afford one now.'

'So that's what this is all about, because I pulled off the big one.'

Lucy stood and held out her hand. 'It doesn't matter, Ernie. Let him watch what he wants. I could do with an early night.'

Ernie's eyes flashed. 'It's our house. You don't have to go to bed early because a guest is unreasonable.'

'Unreasonable! A guest! Is that what I am now?' Colin shook his head.

Lucy looked about to cry. 'Oh, Ernie, don't!'

'You tell him, Lucy. God, I can't believe it! Me own sister's husband giving me a rough time because I want to watch some decent telly for a change.'

Ernie moved as though to leave the room. 'You know there was a fellow in the Army who carried on high and mighty like you. Once we started firing on the Germans, that was the end of him. He copped a bullet from behind.'

Colin jumped up. 'Hit me, go on then, hit me, if it'll get old Green-Eye off your back.'

Ernie shook his head and made for the door. Colin grabbed him.

Lucy moved between the two men and tripped over Colin's outstretched foot. She fell flat on the floor. There was a cracking noise. Both men gasped and went to pick her up.

'Don't touch me!' she screamed.

Sweat dripped down her cheeks and she tried to stand but both wrists dangled uselessly at 90 degree angles and she couldn't make it. Ernie gently put his arms under her shoulders and lifted her onto her feet.

'Look what you've done!' Colin yelled.

Ernie snarled, 'My God, Colin! I could tell you a few facts ...'

Lucy closed her eyes momentarily. 'When you've quite finished,' she said grimly. 'I think I've broken my wrists.'

Ernie stared hard at her wrists. 'I'm taking you to hospital.'

Colin raced to turn off the television. 'I'll come with you.'

'No way! When we get back, I want you gone. I want you, your clothes, everything, out of this house!' He strode over to the mantelpiece, opened an old tea tin and took out the $100 note. 'Here, take what you gave us from your win. Get yourself a room for a few days and build yourself a mansion.'

'But ...'

Ernie helped Lucy to the door. Colin whimpered. 'Lucy, you want me to go with you, don't you?'

His sister shook her head. 'Goodbye, Colin. Let's know your new address.'

Colin flopped down on a sagging bed with its faded quilt and thin mattress. He looked around the sparsely-furnished room that reeked of stale cigarette smoke.

'Bloody ungrateful so-and-sos,' he muttered. 'I could have married any of a dozen widows but I chose to share their patch of the woods. And for what? I strike it lucky, and the old green-eyed monster comes out. A fella can't win against that.' He bounced up and down on the bed. 'And I don't think much of this bed. That hotel bloke downstairs couldn't have recognised me or he'd have done better than this.' A tear trickled down his cheek.

'Doesn't he know a big winner when he sees one?'

The Day I Turned Sixty-Five

Judith A Green

The day before I turned sixty-five, we draped our coats over our arms as we explored Edinburgh Castle – St Margaret's Chapel, the Dog Cemetery, Mons Meg, views through the cannon holes, views from up high, the Great Hall with its splendour and armoury. Our coats saw it all in their gradually scrunched up state. They fulfilled their purpose however, about ten minutes from our Hotel, when the clouds, which had accompanied us most of the day, downloaded.

It was still raining the next morning when we walked from our Hotel. The bus shelter was a welcome respite from the steady downpour. The bus driver explained that the route he was driving didn't go past our destination, the Palace of Holyroodhouse, commonly called Holyrood Palace. However, he would tell us when to get off and how to get there.

'Just cross the road,' he instructed when we arrived at the designated stop. 'Go down to the bridge, cross over and keep walking down the hill. It will take you straight to the entrance to Holyrood Palace.'

It was exactly as the bus driver had said, except, he didn't tell us it was about a three mile walk down the hill. Had we known how far it was we would have sought the shelter of another bus but we kept walking, dodging umbrellas and pedestrians scurrying by with their heads down. One month's rain fell in twenty-four hours, we discovered later.

We finally squelched through the gateway into the grounds of Holyrood Palace, joining the queue of fellow squelchonians into the Gift Shop to buy our tickets. The gardens were closed due to flooding but the Palace was still open. We stood in the rain to take photos, so wet by this stage it didn't worry us. I huddled in a semi-dry, sheltered corner to talk to Number Two son when he rang to wish me a happy birthday. Number One son had already sent me an early morning text.

I always imagine palaces as being ornate, almost ostentatious, but was surprised at the simplicity of Holyrood Palace. Fortunately, the roped-off route visitors must follow was covered by heavy duty plastic, our dripping coats would not harm any of the floor coverings.

I faced great temptation in the first couple of rooms, yearning to reach across the rope barriers to caress the huge wall tapestries created between the 1600's and 1800's depicting specific events in history. They had been woven on large looms by possibly five or six people, most likely men. But it is forbidden to touch that which is so old and fragile. 'I work here,' a staff member on duty laughed when I told her of my yearning, 'but I've never been allowed to touch them either.'

We'd stopped dripping by the time we negotiated the narrow, winding staircases and studied the sad story of Mary, Queen of Scots. I thought of home thousands of miles away. I wouldn't trade it for one ounce of royal wealth or power.

Down the same narrow, winding staircases to the old Abbey built on the site long before Holyrood Palace was built. Four walls, no roof, the original floor long-gone, replaced with a deep layer of white stones, now almost floating in water.

I stand in contemplation under the narrow eaves of the Palace. I don't know how long since the last worship service was held in the Abbey but I always sense a presence, an essence, in ancient ruins. The people are gone but it is as though the spirit of their being lives on in the walls, drifting amongst those who take the time to ponder. I was unaware of those around me until a woman close by echoed my emotions in the words she spoke. I told her I felt the same presence or essence when studying Aboriginal rock art. There was a silence, a quiet, but not emptiness, as those who once walked these places have left the essence of their breathing for us to inhale.

We looked around as our respective husbands joined us, realising we were the only four still in the Abbey. 'They've closed the Abbey,' my just-met-companion's husband said. 'Someone slipped on the walkway. We don't have to hurry out, they're just not letting anyone else in.'

A young Scotsman dressed in a traditional kilt stood by the entrance. I felt sorry for him standing there on a wet, thirteen degree day with a brisk breeze blowing. Whatever he may or may not be wearing under his kilt, it would still be a chilly sensation in his nether regions. I quickly admonished myself. These were hardly appropriate thoughts in the confines of this ancient Abbey! The young Scotsman bid us a friendly farewell.

We caught a bus up the hill. It wasn't going on the route we needed but the kindly bus driver told us the correct stop to alight at. We crossed the bridge, walked along the street until we reached the bus stop on the route we needed to return to the Hotel. We were fortunate to be able to wait beneath the bus shelter.

Stepping aboard the bus we were greeted by a cheery, 'Did you find the Palace okay?' It was the same bus driver who had directed us that morning.

'We did,' we chorused. 'But we got a tad damp along the way.' Water dripped from our coat hoods down our faces. Drips circled our feet from the bottoms of our coats.

'Oh aye,' he replied, the outer edges of his eyes crinkling ever-so-slightly as the corners of his mouth curled upwards. 'Oh aye.'

Brain Tumour

Rebecca Maxwell

losing language,
bruising friendships,
a chasm between thought and expression!
who knows where you are,
who knows where you have been since yesterday,
who knows, with this drain between feeling and word.

how shall I meet you?
how shall I show you I still know the real you?

how to convey there are friends who ask about you,
the many who remember your past, and still care?

how can I soothe the pain of your prison?
how can I soften the knot of your night?
how can I assure you
the locked doors of the present will open
into spiritual reality and light.

and now I remember you twofold:
the distorted victim of bodily cancer,
and the olden-time generous and capable friend.

still, like the real being of each of us
you are always a tone in the music of God.

Alone Time

Vanessa Story

Third place in the Kathryn Purnell Poetry Prize, 2019

An om of air fills my lungs.
Eyes closed; body relaxed.
A brief respite of me.
Seconds weighed as hours,
Immersed in a fragile sanctuary.

A tremor in my mini universe.
In the distance, growing louder,
The sound of feet and claws.
A terrible hunt has begun,
Panting, scratching towards the door.

I tense, holding myself still,
As if my stillness will be enough
To hold the universe in stillness too.

There is a pause, a re-evaluation,
A listening for something new.
A cross-species consultation.

I take a diver's breath.
Lungs burning, eyes squeezing tighter shut.

The noise begins again, scuttling near,
Quickening its pace,
Heavy panting; closing on the deer.

I panic. I reveal my inner desperation.
My voice taken from me,
I try to suppress a cough.
The smallest of sounds escapes,
And it is more than enough.

A victory roaring in the air,
The door flies open,
An eruption of fur and skin,
A tussle to devour me first.
The pack closing in.
Arms circle my waist,
A head buries into my side,
Squealing in delight
At the discovery of me,
Face shining with winner's pride.
Two paws plant on my shoulders.
A furry head thrusts towards mine,
Desperate to be acknowledged
As the favourite child,
Longing for a before time.

I accept my fate and hand my body back
To its rightful owners.
I stand up, flush the toilet,
Wash my hands in the correct way,
And allow myself to be led away.

Kitty's Ivory Lover

Maribel Steele

Published in Outsider Art Magazine, *Issue Two, 2014*

He had always said it didn't bother him she was blind. In fact, he had laughed, 'You're the perfect partner for me, Kitty-babe.'

'Hmm?' She smiled.

He unravelled a thin yellow ribbon from his shirt pocket, and wound it gently around her ring finger. 'Yeah. No other woman I've been with can walk past a jeweller's window like you do.' Placing his soft lips on Kitty's fourth finger he added, 'Save this one for me, OK?'

Kitty fumbles to unlock the front door. Her scarf catches on the cactus plant he had bought from some dodgy second-hand shop on the not-so-fashionable side of Chapel Street. She jabs the key into the lock, rips the yellow ribbon from her ring finger, and hurls the white cane down the corridor. She slams the door as hard as she can. *How dare he!*

A crystal vase wobbles on the hall table as Kitty thunders past, knocking over the sagging red flowers he had given her. Shards of glass explode across the tiled floor. She crushes fragments of glass and petals under her black boots.

Moving around the bedroom, her hands stray over every surface in search of anything he may have left behind. It was all going in the bin. Hands sift through empty drawers and cupboards. She finds nothing. Kitty kneels on the shaggy rug on his side of the bed, and burrows madly underneath the low futon, her hands delighted to have found something of his she can shred to pieces. A pile of magazines, or *The Financial Review*, no doubt.

He liked to scan through the pages as she lay next to him in bed, curled up and purring: with limbs intertwined and hands moving over each other's salty-skin. He assured her it was important to keep an eye on rising trends in the stock market.

Kitty launches the magazines into the air one by one, aiming for the rubbish bin, none of them making it to the target. An assortment of papers litter the room. *Prick!* she curses, and gathers the papers up.

A glossy photo on the front cover makes her take a closer look. Her tear-filled eyes widen, travelling carefully over the black font two inches from her face. Bold, lush, defiant – *PLAYBOY*. What else had she not seen?

Outside the window, a pair of nesting doves wake her from her thoughts as they coo, *You fool, you fool.*

'Shut up!'

The love birds continue their torment. Heat rises into her cheeks and she hurls his pillow at the window. The smell of his sandalwood cologne makes her feel sick. In the early days of their relationship, his irresistible scent had comforted her as she lay awake, wondering how a man could truly love a woman who was going blind.

She craved to experience intimacy as a whole woman – not partially-sighted – and it hurt to think how he would be limited by choosing a woman who couldn't connect through visual body language.

Kitty wanted to prove to herself that she was more than vision-impaired. She knew how to bounce back when she suffered embarrassment: bumping into street poles, tripping over children, falling into holes, bruising shins and ego. Laughing at misfortune had become a way of life.

Kitty had honed her wits to get out of sticky situations, accidentally walking over wet cement, jumping a queue and then ordering without a ticket, knocking items off a shelf, wearing odd-coloured shoes. He went along with the humorous aspects of Kitty's blind life, teasing her.

'Pity, babe, you can't see how good looking I am!'

They laughed that there were never any arguments about who had the car for the weekend, and he loved that she never gave him directions when they drove in his make-believe Porsche.

But the day he announced he was moving interstate and thought it best they go their separate ways was the day he confessed he couldn't face another divorce – two ex-wives had pulled the financial rug from underneath him. He wasn't willing to risk a third marriage with any woman, no matter how much he loved her.

In the fading pink evening light, the piano sits in the corner of the living room like a reassuring friend, calling to Kitty, *Come. Come and play me.* She returns to the only lover who had never betrayed her. Her mood softens as she moves closer to the iron-framed piano, her tightened brow replaced by the trace of a small smile.

Fingers slip into the spaces between keys, spread elegantly, wings over middle C.

She shifts in the seat, hands diving for the lower register to strike at the keys, thumping out discordant tones while her foot stomps on the pedal.

Thoughts and fragments of their conversations jump into her mind as Kitty's hands randomly twist and turn over the octaves. The wooden hammers with their felt claws strike the strings beneath the lid of the piano, each dampened thud echoes her troubled heart, *Why did he leave?*

Hands quiver, shoulders release and her tightened throat prepares for sobbing. Safe in the intimacy of free expression, her heart opens into a space where she can let go of unfulfilled promises.

Salty tears trace a course down Kitty's cheeks and trembling hands. Thoughts seek shelter from the words, *Let go, let go, let go.* The music plays on, dancing through Kitty's fingers, lifting her heart above the maze of self-doubt.

Hours later, she is cradled in warmth between letting go and acceptance. Her heart is captivated by the music. Ecstasy flows through every part of her being.

Fading chords linger in the room as moonlight peers through the curtains. She hears the long deep breaths escape from her lips. Placing a moist kiss on her open palm, Kitty pats down on the warm keys of her ivory lover and gently closes the wooden lid.

A smile breaks free, and Kitty promises to replace the broken vase in the light of a new day. The flowers this time will come from her own garden.

The Devil Doesn't Play Fair

Paula Wilson

The Devil doesn't play fair. Some people say the Devil doesn't exist. I was one of them. That changed on November 24. There I was broken down in the middle of the Simpson Desert. I was going to die, that was for sure. Four-wheel drive given up the ghost, except for steam hissing from the motor. Water-supply non-existent. Mobile phone dead as Moses.

I let the last of the water drop on my tongue and hurled the bottle to the ground. Maybe I could drink water from the radiator. Too late. All steam had ceased and rusty water no longer dripped onto the sand. All that remained was a damp patch that was rapidly drying up. I looked up at the sun – must have been at least 42 degrees. Looked like I was definitely going the way of my phone and joining Moses.

Moses was an alright guy, he saved a lot of people. If I prayed, maybe he'd save me. Not that I believed in God or any of those Bible guys. They belonged on the same imaginary planet as the Devil. But just maybe. Maybe Moses was the man to call out to.

So, I'm slumped in the shade of the vehicle, trying to figure out the words you say to a guy who died a few thousand years ago and might well be the product of a very clever writer's imagination.

'Dear Moses …'

'Hey Moses, how about some help here?'

'Moses, if you can just come and work a little magic ...' Maybe not, he might be offended if I call his stuff magic.

'Moses, if you could just see your way to helping me out of this situation, I promise ...'

I thought I was hallucinating, but the sound got louder and nearer.

I'm on my feet trying to figure out which direction it's coming from, the sound seems to be closing in on me from all directions. I'm swinging circles, checking the sky. Nothing.

'Looks like you're in a spot of bother,' a voice boomed in my ear. I twirl around to find a black leather-clad bloke on an equally black motorbike.

'Moses?' I couldn't see a long white beard but it had to be Moses.

'Well, what do you promise?'

'I'm not sure,' I reply, shaking my head.

'How about if I get you out of this mess you become one of my disciples?'

'I didn't know you had disciples. I thought they belonged to Jesus.'

'We all have some form of disciples in this business.'

It didn't take much thinking, being one of Moses's disciples doing good stuff? I could handle that.

'You're on,' I reply, sticking out my hand.

'Deal,' he said, and we shake on it.

It was while he had a firm grip on my hand that I saw movement behind him. Walking towards us was an old guy with a long white beard and wearing robes. I stepped back from Moses. He turned towards the oncoming man.

'You're too late again,' he yelled.

'You been up to your tricks again, Lucifer?'

'Lucifer?' I backed into my vehicle.

'Moses, you really need to update your mode of transport.' The motorcyclist pulled off his helmet and revealed a head of shaggy black hair with two small pointy bits sticking up. Horns! He had horns!

'You're not Moses?' I said.

'I never claimed to be,' he laughed and gestured towards the old guy. 'Sam, meet Moses.'

Moses dipped his head in my direction, 'Maybe I should upgrade.' He ran his hand over the motorbike. 'Next time Lucifer.' With that he walked back into the desert.

That's how I ended up working for the Devil. Instead of doing good stuff, I'm causing havoc. Not so much havoc; more like mischief.

It's just past midnight, I'm going to be busy today because the Devil and his disciples don't play fair.

Especially on Christmas day.

Families Drift

Rebecca Maxwell

like autumn leaves,
family members drift,
fall away, drift away beyond reach.
and the dry bereft trees of our garden
continue living, though more naked,
less shielded,
touched by a long, long, winter.

then some hopes of spring resurge,
whispering the hope of possible contact –
perhaps renewed relating,

the intent of winter's cold forgotten.

fresh perspectives do take shape,
with mutual good will,
and slowly, slowly.
the journey of growth and unfolding
may be experienced again,
experienced newly, and softly.

can we trust the optimistic idiom,
that hope springs eternal,
and that it bodes the renewal of warmth?

The Vigil

Leigh Hay

The child seemed listless. An uncharacteristic lethargy had stilled his small body these last two days. The youngest of five, Hugh made it his purpose in life to keep pace with his older brothers. But today, he curled in a chair, disinclined to move a muscle. Nessie was certain that Hugh was sickening for something. She checked his temperature, grateful that the older boys were at school and her youngest could rest quietly. Nessie returned to the washtub to finish soaking collars and cuffs: Alf's clerical robes needed refreshing.

On doctor's advice, Alf had reluctantly requested a change of parish. Plagued by bouts of bronchitis, a warmer, drier climate would promote more robust health, assured the local physician. The quiet, leafy Adelaide Hills reminded Alf of Kent and the old country and the thought of moving further north held little appeal. Originally from Leicester, Alf had never quite made the successful transition to this land where the seasons were wrong. However, within weeks of requesting a transfer, the family packed up house and belongings in Gumeracha and journeyed by bus, train and finally horse drawn cart to Laura in the mid-north region of South Australia. Their arrival was noted in the local newspaper, particularly as the new pastor and his wife had five children to augment the twenty enrolled at the primary school. Miss Ethel Jacobs, the Sunday School Superintendent, was heard to say how pleased she was that the Long children would boost numbers at Victoria Street Baptist.

The child pushed away the glass of water that his mother offered him. His cheeks were flushed and he had begun to cough and was having difficulty swallowing. His temperature was high and when questioned, he replied in a hoarse little voice that his head hurt. Nessie checked for tell-tale signs of measles or chicken pox. If one child was infected, she would simply put them all into bed together and deal with the contagion in one fell swoop. Whatever Hugh was coming down with, Nessie would cope as she always did, in her capable, practical way.

Nessie's brood was thick as thieves and twice as devious. Hugh idolised William, the eldest, and would do anything he asked of him. For his part, William specialised in winding up his naïve youngest brother and watch as Hugh was reprimanded. The property of the Baptist church, *Morris House* was not equipped for raucous antics, but try telling that to five energetic children. Alf's pulpit voice frequently echoed down the corridor, '*Nessie … the children must play outside … I'm trying to write …*' In dulcet tones, Nessie would encourage the boys to play elsewhere – the stable if it was raining – and when her initial polite requests were ignored, she bribed them with biscuits, followed by threats and finally a wooden spoon to chase them through the back door.

Nessie would be lying to say her youngest wasn't her favourite, but, as much as she doted on her baby, Nessie would nevertheless be pleased when he too finally went off to the local school. She would have more time to help Alf run the parish. The house and church were situated less than two miles from the one room, timber school. Gideon Gardner was a mature, no-nonsense teacher with many years' experience. He was strict and could manage the combined ages effectively. In the brief visits Nessie made to the school, she'd been impressed with Gideon's empathy and kindness to his pupils. She liked to think he'd had a Christian upbringing, although she was yet to see him at Sunday service. That was providing he was Protestant of course. If he happened to be Catholic, she doubted they would have much in common.

To the delight of the Long children, *Morris House* came complete with a stable and an agreeable pony. The pony quickly acquired the name of *Abee* and within weeks of their arrival, was nosing the kitchen door for Nessie to feed him carrots or apples. The family also acquired a horse for the buggy as well as a cow. Hugh loved nothing more than playing in the semi-wilderness of the back garden. He climbed, ran, crawled on all fours, dug copious roads and built dirt ramps for his racetracks. He was fascinated by, indeed fixated on, anything with wheels. Up until two days ago, the little boy had been a bundle of pent up exuberance and wild imagination.

As the afternoon progressed, so did the cough. By six that night, Hugh's breathing was laboured.

'Alf, I think we should send for Doctor Fothergill.' Alf looked up from his newspaper. 'Is he ill enough for that?'

Nessie understood Alf's reticence at the thought of harnessing the horse and riding into town to summon the only doctor for fifty miles. Old Fothergill was not always amiable, depending on the time of day or the number of patients he was required to attend. He also cherished his mealtimes and if gossip was to be believed, a shot or two of malt whisky.

Nessie could be forthright when the occasion demanded. 'Yes, Hugh is sufficiently ill, Alf. Just listen to his breathing.'

Alf rose from the easy chair, folded the paper with a sigh, and strode across the room. He bent over his youngest and gently turned the tiny face towards him. The limp body neither met his gaze nor responded to his touch. Having been absent all afternoon, Alf had not witnessed Hugh's rapid decline.

'We need Fothergill right away.' And with that, the tall, elegant man made for the stable with haste. 'Keep my supper hot!'

Supper would have to wait. The children could make do with bread and jam. Nessie's priority was Hugh and she bustled to the kitchen for the wide bowl she used for scalding milk and half filled it with cold water. She fossicked in the linen press until she found the torn strips of old sheeting, soaked them in the water and sponged her child's fevered brow. She had to bring Hugh's temperature down.

What was taking Alf so long? Nessie had been watching the mantle clock for nearly an hour.

At the sound of footsteps, Nessie ran to the door.

'Is Doctor Fothergill with you?' she whispered to Alf.

'Following close behind.'

Within minutes, Alf was ushering the doctor through the kitchen to the hastily assembled trundle bed where Hugh lay fighting for breath.

The doctor came straight to the point. 'How long has he been like this?'

'Since this morning.'

Skilled fingers explored swelling in Hugh's neck, and with a quick look at the boy's throat, he asked, 'And the illness has progressed rapidly?'

Nessie shot a quick look in Alf's direction. 'Yes, very … what do you think it is?'

'I don't think, Mrs Long, I know. The boy has diphtheria. I've heard there's an epidemic in Victoria but this is the first case in our local district.'

At this revelation, Nessie froze. Diphtheria meant death.

'There's no time to lose,' said Doctor Fothergill, 'the boy has laryngeal diphtheria and if I don't insert a tube into his larynx soon he will quite simply suffocate.'

Nessie sprang into action.

'What do you need?'

'Nothing,' replied the doctor. 'I have a scalpel, and tube and if you would both leave the room, this won't take long. I'll call you when I've finished.'

Within minutes, Nessie and Alf were summoned by the doctor. The sound of Hugh's rasping had diminished, thanks to the rubber tube protruding from his larynx.

'I've performed an emergency procedure called tracheotomy,' said the doctor. 'The tube must be kept in place, swabbed and kept clean. I have also removed some of the dead tissue starting to line his throat. The next twenty-four hours are crucial.'

Nessie opened her mouth to speak, but Doctor Fothergill wasn't finished.

'The other children are not to go anywhere near Hugh. Diphtheria is highly contagious. Hugh will need weeks of bed rest, fluids, soft food and no physical exertion. Is that understood?'

Nessie nodded.

'And you must both wash your hands after tending to Hugh. I will call back tomorrow to check on him.'

With a professional flourish, Fothergill departed as abruptly as he had entered. Nessie let Alf see him out and returned to kneel beside Hugh's hot, semi-conscious body. She bathed his brow, inspected the tube entry and bent closer to make sure he was indeed still breathing. She pulled a low chair adjacent to the bed and, when Alf returned, asked him to fetch her woollen shawl. There was no way she would be leaving her child's side. Not now, not in an hour's time, not even by morning. Sleep was out of the question. Nessie would not take her eyes off her son. He must survive and to do that, she must be vigilant.

Doctor Fothergill returned on the following days to check on his patient. On his third visit, he removed the tube, applied a tiny stitch and dressed the small incision in the neck. He assured Nessie it would heal in time. The possible source of the infection remained unknown. Hugh was still the only case in the district. The child was not yet at school and his brothers were not ill, so they could not be the source. As the only practicing doctor, Fothergill didn't relish the thought of an epidemic on his hands.

Confined to barracks, the Long boys worked enthusiastically on their story ... *and Hugh was suffocating! Dr Fothergill put this rubber tube down Hugh's throat ... and suddenly he could breathe again!* 'Tracheotomy' was difficult to pronounce, let alone spell, but in the grand scheme of storytelling, it didn't matter. Their brother had almost died. Which other kid could top that one? They couldn't wait to return to school.

After days and nights of bedside vigil, Nessie finally fell into an exhausted sleep in the chair. Alf bundled up her slight body and carried her to their bed. She would not wake for twelve hours.

When she stirred, groggy and with a raging thirst, her first thought was of Hugh. How could Alf have let her sleep? She lumbered from the bedroom, weaving her way along the corridor on still shaky legs, calling for her husband. Passing his study, she saw that Alf was calmly engrossed in yet another sermon. This was utterly incomprehensible!

'Alf… why aren't you with Hugh?'

Alf raised his eyes to meet his wife's admonishment.

'Hugh has improved, dear. And he's being well looked after.'

Nessie blinked, and reached for the door jamb for support. What a ridiculous statement to make. If Alf wasn't tending to their son, who on Earth was?

The sitting room was sunny, with a refreshing breeze from a door open to the verandah. A pale Hugh, propped on the trundle by two large pillows, was playing quietly with his tin cars. Perched on the end of the bed was William, sharing his toys, speaking gently and ensuring Hugh lacked for nothing.

'William? What are you doing? You'll catch diphtheria!'

Both boys turned toward their mother woman standing in the doorway. Hugh managed a small smile.

'You were sleeping and Father was tired,' answered William. 'Anyway, I don't mind looking after my brother.'

While Nessie slept, William stayed by Hugh's bedside until he could stay awake no longer. Alf had carried him to bed, only to find him back with Hugh at the first opportunity.

No-one, including Fothergill, would ever discover who infected Hugh. William would contract diphtheria, but not as seriously as his brother. Once word got around that Hugh and William were ill, and that Hugh had been miraculously saved by Fothergill at the eleventh hour, the parishioners rallied with food. Billies of soup, vegetables, live chickens and cakes were deposited on the back step, with a knock to announce their arrival. No-one would enter *Morris House* for fear of infection. To Alf's constant irritation, the quarantined Long boys ran amok.

For years Hugh slept on the open verandah and whenever possible, went without shoes. This, Doctor Fothergill maintained, would help toughen him up. Hugh's passion for cars never waned. He grew up loving his mother but would forever love his brother more.

Those Germans From The Pottery

Janice Williams

A earlier version of this story was awarded first place in the Wimmera Regional Library Writing Competition, 2015

'I'm home, Mum,' called Nell. She unpinned her hat, and tutted as her soft brown hair tumbled down, billowing to her waist. It always did that, despite apprentice tailors of sixteen having to keep their hair tidy.

'How was work?' asked Annie Fischer. The voice was bright enough. But Nell noticed that her mother's eyes remained lowered over the khaki balaclava she was knitting.

'Not bad,' replied Nell. 'There's a pageant for the Red Cross Comfort Fund, and Mrs Grant – you know, with the red hair – is to be Queen Elizabeth. She's ordered a dress with a grey silk bodice stiffened like armour, and silver sequins all over the skirt. I guess I know who'll be sewing the sequins!' Her mother looked up; that was when Nell saw her red eyes. 'Mum, what's up? Not Maurice?'

'No.' Annie dabbed her eyes. 'I went shopping, and it was rather nasty.'

'Were you refused service again?'

'Yes, in two shops. And that la-de-da Mrs Vincent pushed past me in a doorway, and said she wouldn't be kept waiting by "those Germans from the pottery". But it wasn't as bad as Mr Patterson saying I was sleeping with a dirty Boche.'

'Mum, no!' Nell's cheeks burned with indignation.

'Yes. This war is dreadful enough, without being intimidated because your father's parents were German.'

'But they came out last century,' retorted Nell. 'Dad's as good an Australian as anyone.'

'Of course. But they're saying we should be interned in case we are spies. Did you ever hear anything so wrong and sinful?'

Nell's flush reached the roots of her fine hair. 'They couldn't, could they?'

'No, it's wicked spite. Sometimes I feel like a prisoner in my own home. That horrid Albie Briggs spat at me yesterday.'

'Oh Mum, Maurice would thrash him blue –' She bit her lip. Her brother Maurice had been fighting in France for a year. Who knew how things were? 'Anyway, Albie's aim is terrible,' she ended weakly. She pushed back her unruly hair, fighting her miserable reflections.

Sixteen months ago, they had thought the victimisation was a short bout of unpleasantness. But it was December 1916, and there were still outbreaks. Like a recurring disease, Nell thought, bad war news making it flare again. Still, there were unexpected kindnesses. Last week, on Dad's birthday, a fruit cake mysteriously appeared on the doorstep with a note: 'Best wishes, George Adolph.' Everyone called Dad that. Probably it was Mrs Patterson: her cakes were prize-winners. She was the wife of their worst persecutor; but they ate the cake and left the plate out with some home-grown apricots. The plate and the apricots disappeared overnight.

The clock struck six. Her mother sprang up. 'Teatime, and I'm here moping. Annie Fischer, you should be ashamed of yourself,' she scolded herself.

'What can I do?' asked Nell.

'I just have to thicken the stew. Go and change. And tie up your hair. Young Bill Nelson would think it pretty, I'm sure, but you don't want it falling in your food.'

Nell changed her work dress, thinking of Maurice, Bill, and their schoolmates at the Front. Stupid that people in this town blamed her family for this stupid war! She picked up a letter from Maurice, worn with reading.

Dear everyone,

Thanks for sox and gloves. Weather is cold, but action hot. Tell Nell I saw her boy in London on leave. We went to Madame Tussaud's. The waxworks were so lifelike. We will go together one day.

Months ago, that was!

'Hurry, Nellie,' called Annie. 'Your father's here.'

George Adolph was brushing clay particles from his bushy handlebar moustache. Clay clung to him even when he dressed for church: as though Fischers' Pottery & Brickworks rubbed into his very skin. Nell wondered if Grandfather George, whom she never knew, had carried the Pottery under his nails like Dad.

A little girl of four tugged her skirt. 'H'llo, Auntie Nellie.'

Nell stroked her niece's dark hair. 'Hello, Millie. Are you sleeping here tonight?'

'Mmm. Mummy's tired. She'll be better when the doctor brings the baby, I 'spect.'

'I 'spect – expect so,' Nell corrected. Millie was here most days. Even sixteen-year-old Nell knew her sister Bessie's pregnancy was not going well. 'Come and sit beside me.' They all bowed their heads as George Adolph said grace.

'What have you been doing, Millie?' asked Nell.

'Helping Grandpa in the pottery. I made little clay men, and he put them in the kiln. They are soldiers, and my dolly is going to nurse them better. Will you make her a nurse's dress?' she asked hopefully.

'With a veil and a red cape,' agreed Nell.

'And I watched Grandpa paint the sign over the pottery.' She giggled. 'He left "C" out. He spelt it "F-I-S-H-E-R" like a fisherman.'

Nell smiled. 'How did you know?'

'I know lots of words. I start school next year.' She licked her spoon complacently. 'I know "HUN". It was on the wall, but Grandpa painted it out.'

There was a sticky silence. 'If you've finished, you can get those patty cakes we made from the pantry,' said Annie. 'Don't drop them.'

Millie left, and Annie turned to her husband. 'Are we driven to change our name now, George Adolph?'

Nell noticed how determined her father's square chin could be. 'I thought about it. But it would be like glazing a cracked pot. The whole town knows my family was German. We'll face this thing out!' He slammed his fist, making the crockery jump. 'I'll paint "Fischer" back.'

Millie returned, carrying the cake plate. 'Are you cross, Grandpa?'

'Not with you, poppet.' He picked her up and tickled her face with his moustache. She squirmed deliciously.

'Tell me a story. Please?'

George Adolph was a famous storyteller. Nell recalled one where his moustache was turned into a caterpillar by a fairy. He stroked Millie's dark mane. 'I'll tell you how the pottery started, pet. Years ago, my father lived in a place called Bavaria.'

'Where is that?'

'In Germany.'

'Mr Patterson says Germans are bad. Was he bad?'

'No. He worked very hard. He was a potter.'

'Like you?'

'Yes. He made beautiful pots. He threw them on the wheel, and a pot grew up, smooth and even. Then he fired them.'

'Like you, with my little men.'

'Who's telling this? He decorated them with flowers and birds, and glazed them shiny bright.'

'As good as yours?'

'Even better.'

'Don't 'spect they were.'

Nell thought of the lovely flower-encrusted jug and basin on her washstand. Dad had made it for her birthday, hours of careful work by a master potter. Even Dad said he'd never made better.

'Stop interrupting. He married a lady called Celestina, and they left for Australia.'

'Why?'

'Germany was poor then. It was said that in Australia you could pick up gold like pebbles. They got on a ship –'

'Like Uncle Maurice?'

'That was a steamship. In the olden days they had great ships with billowing sails. Trips took months. There were storms, and passengers got seasick. But they reached Australia at last. A shipping man asked my father's name, and he said "Johannes Georg Fischer". But his accent was so thick, and Germans say "Gey-org". The man wrote down "George", and that was his name ever after.'

'And you are George 'Dolph. Did he find gold?'

'No. The surface gold was gone. People had to tunnel through hard quartz rock. George dug a shaft in a place where the ground was clay. Potters can make things from clay that new towns need – bricks, tiles, pipes. He started a little pottery. A horse walked around in a circle, stirring clay and turning the rollers.'

'Poor horse!'

'Oh, Whitey was well looked after. I was a little boy, and my job was to feed him hay. Not oats, mind, as he'd get frisky, and the clay would go lumpy.' Millie chuckled. 'The pottery grew.

Poor German men would come, and George gave them work. By the time Vater Gott 'took him to heaven, I was the potter. And Fischers' Pottery is still going. Now, *you* are to go to bed.'

Millie made her round of kisses, and trotted down the passage. 'Brush your teeth,' called Nell. 'I'll come and tuck you in.'

Annie stacked dishes in the sink. 'I'll wash up if you're to make dolls' clothes, Nellie. George Adolph, how *are* things going with the pottery?' The story's spell dissolved. Gloom settled again.

'Not good,' he admitted. 'Sales are down. They're bad times. We can't help it.'

'No,' agreed Annie. 'But it's not the bad times. It's being treated like a pariah in our own town.' She swished the soap around as if it had done her a personal spite.

Nell was cutting into an old skirt, slashing like a sword with the shears. It was bad technique, but it felt satisfying. 'I hate this narrow-minded town –'

The doorknocker clattered, and George Adolph went to open. 'Albie!'

It was the spitting boy, now in postal uniform. 'Tallygrum, Mr Fischer.'

Telegram! Nell felt sick. Her father reached out, his hand shaking. Albie actually saluted.

George Adolph read: 'REGRET TO INFORM YOU PTE MAURICE B FISCHER WOUNDED RIGHT ARM DETAILS TO FOLLOW.'

'He's alive, anyway,' breathed Nell. But so little information. Wounds could lead to anything: gangrene, amputation, septicaemia.

George Adolph blew his nose doggedly. 'You can't kill Maurice. Remember when he fell eight feet from that tree? He was a mess, but he –'

His observation was cut short by the phone ringing. Nell leapt as though Maurice might be calling. 'Fischers' Pottery –'

'Bloody Huns. Baby killers!' The line went dead.

'Who's that?' The receiver trembled in Nell's hand. 'Dad, did you hear?'

Her father snatched the receiver. 'I heard. This has gone too far. Hello, Exchange? Someone put through an offensive call just now. I believe the police take these things seriously.'

The telephonist stammered. 'Aw, Mr Fischer, I dunno. I was on another call.'

'Really? Well, whatever the case, you can tell future anonymous callers that my son Maurice has been wounded fighting for the Empire.' He hung up with a clatter.

'George Adolph, it will be all over the district.'

'Good. Put the kettle on, we could do with some tea.'

The kettle had barely boiled when the knocker banged. Nell ran to the door. 'Mrs Patterson!'

'I brought a fruit cake, dear,' their neighbour gabbled. 'A bit's cut off, but I told Col you'd need it if you had droppers-in. I just heard about Maurice.' It was obvious how she'd heard. She radiated defiance. *Let* Mr Patterson complain about his lost cake!

'Th-thank you. Would you like some tea?'

'Wouldn't say no.'

Mrs Patterson was in full flight over her tea, ('Don't worry, Maurice is tough. Remember his fall from the plum tree?' she kept insisting), when more neighbours arrived. Nell hurried to the door.

'Mum, it's the Gillespies.'

Mrs Gillespie pushed a steak pie at her. 'I had it in the meat safe. It might save your mum some work. We heard about Maurice.'

Her daughter Lou simpered. 'What a mercy Maurice didn't have face wounds. He's so handsome.' Nell just nodded. Lou couldn't help being stupid.

The knocker went again, this time Reverend Wallace. His shoulders were stooped with the weight of many such calls. 'I heard about Maurice. But you're busy. I'll come again.'

George Adolph drew him in. 'No, Reverend. Vater Gott has sent you. Nell, get another cup, the good china from the crystal cabinet.'

Nell was fetching it when a little ghost in a white ruffled nightie appeared. 'You said you'd tuck me in,' Millie reproached.

'Millie, I'm sorry, I forgot.'

'Is there a party?'

'Yes – no – sort of. Uncle Maurice is hurt. People have come to be kind to us.'

Millie took her hand. 'When I'm a big girl, I will nurse Uncle Maurice better.'

'When you're a big girl there won't be war, or men being hurt.' Nell cuddled her, careful not to drop the cup and saucer. No, the potter's wheel would have turned. They would study war no more.

Postscript: I closed the family history, mentally hugging the child Millie that my mother-in-law had been.

Organic Gardening

Trudy Oldaker

Winner of the ABC Gardening Australia competition, 2001
Published in Bird Brains *by Trudy Oldaker, 2019*

Digging, planting untarnished soil,
Vitamin bursting, reaping toil,
Ladybirds, songbirds chasing foes:
Healthier old age – fewer woes!

The House Is Gone

Judith A Green

Highly Commended in the Kathryn Purnell Poetry Prize, 2019

once over the cattle grid it is a straight line to the house
past the paddock then
between the trees shading the used-to-be-blacksmith's shed
and the plantation of native trees
as the driveway approaches the house surrounded
by a white ant proof corrugated iron fence
it curves
past the wrought iron front gate only strangers use
on the left
and the peppercorn tree laden with pink morsels
home to the cat-attacking willie wagtails
on the right
then it stops
at the iron and mesh back gate
door bell squealing in its opening and banging shut
the path from the back gate to the house
braces itself
for farmers stamping their boots
removing seasonal attachments
warning Mum alone

no stranger comes
the dogs in coded barks have already signalled
a stranger bark or Dad bark
when sun dims its lights
snarling, gutteral possums
perform on the roof theatre
on the western side
canvas blinds
reject late afternoon heat
on moonless nights
as stars pinprick briquette-coloured skies
invading monsters sideways trampoline
off their still warm surfaces
into the pencil pines
either side of the steps
leading to the front door only strangers knock at
attempt to sidle through the gap
between door and frame
repelled by the threats of a gentle Mum
murmuring to a frightened child
how she'll keep the monsters at bay
with her frying pan

the space
where the house once stood
is infused
with what my eyes can no longer see

Metamorphosis

Margaret Pearce

I opened the window and looked out. The night suited my mood. It was black outside. I was black inside.

The rain poured down like sighing beads. Drops glistened as they fell past the light from the window, and the air was damp and perfumed with raw earth and gum trees.

A wind of discontent stirred the blackness inside me, stirred it like the occasional gust shook the trees outside.

Beneath the yellow glow from the lampshade the room appeared tawdry and shabby; scuffed mat, yuck pink coloured, crumpled bed, pillow wet with tears. My tears. The dressing table was filled with the clutter of my mucked up life. Four toppled birthday cards. My cuddly doll with the stuffing gone from one arm lay across three love letters from Geoff, next to spilt green nail polish and the last of the mascara.

"Why green nail polish?" 'She' had wailed.

Was I thirteen only yesterday? My doll, tea set and fairy-tale books belonged to yesterday. Yesterday was such a secure age. An age away.

Mascara, green nail polish and love letters belonged to tomorrow. I didn't belong in tomorrow. I was pretending when I stepped across yesterday to tomorrow.

I was a fraud and a phoney and nobody guessed. Balancing across that fearsome gulf I was scared yellow, and nobody knew. I was in my own no-man's land.

I examined the reflection in the mirror. "Mirror, Mirror on the wall, tell me who I am at all?"

Short hair and heavily determined features. Boy or girl? Thirteen for a boy was a wide-open adventure. Strong shoulders and square capable hands that could hit a ball straighter and further than anyone else. No waist or hips. Thirteen for a girl was lousy. They weren't allowed to run free like a boy. I didn't want to be sheltered, protected, and kept under lock and key like a caged animal.

The thought of locks brought back the family brawl in all its squalor. Presiding over the accusations and counter accusations, 'She' uncomprehending, stupid and unjust, and 'It' shocked and equally uncomprehending.

"Your horse is costing us a lot of money. The least you can do is be grateful for what you've got, and more understanding about how hard it is to manage."

"The horse didn't cost you, you pair of phonies!" I shouted. Maybe I shouldn't have yelled but I was mad. "You got a nice little nest egg from the sale of the old house. The saddle is a bargain at five hundred dollars. You could find the money if you wanted to. I can't believe you're so tight-fisted!"

Just one day after turning thirteen, to be punished like an eleven-year-old for telling the oldies a few facts of life. It wasn't fair. It wasn't fair at all.

The house is quiet. No television or wireless murmuring. 'She' and 'It' must have gone to bed. There was just the sound of the rain as it gurgled and pattered on the leaves and dripped past my window. The sound cooled and soothed the hot blackness churning inside me.

I stuffed two pillows under my bedcovers and placed the cuddly doll where my head should be. Artistic really, with one pillow twisted to look like a hip. I checked my bedroom door was tightly shut and switched off the light.

The windowsill was slippery. I climbed out and dropped onto the wet soft ground below and collected my bridle from under the house. The night was a strange new kingdom. The streetlights were blurry halos, and the road a shining black ribbon.

Every step I took into the night changed me. I was no longer poised in a no-man's land. I was neither young nor old, neither boy nor girl. The blackness freed me. I was me.

My hair plastered down over my eyes, clung to my neck and dripped the warm rain down my back. My runners squelched and softened to a sensitive extra skin. I felt the grittiness of the mud, and the roundness of the pebbles in the murmuring gutters.

I picked up half a brick and threw it, exultation at the extra energy flowing through me. The streetlight gave a distant apologetic pop, the sound smothered by the darkness that spread as it broke.

The lane was a black tunnel. I flew along with like a bat. I hurdled the fence and ran down the paddock towards the formless blur of Bill.

Bill was warm and wonderful and smelled of sun warmed hay.

My breathing eased. I was comforted. There was just the soft rain, the black night and the horse, my horse, with his sympathetic nostrils, acceptance and tolerance in each forward flick of his ears.

I was thirteen. Summer was over and my summer was gone forever. Forever was a lifetime. I hugged Bill so hard that the beat of his heart drummed through me.

B-boom, b-boom it went, an insistent and instantly soothing drum. I buckled on the bridle and sprang onto the horse's back. The heat of Bill's body and the rain welded my knees to its side. Bill broke into a trot, a canter, and then a flat-out gallop for the fence.

We jumped. The power of the jump surged through me as Bill hurtled over. It was like flying. It felt as if I had plunged over a waterfall half and was swimming, half-flying through insubstantial mist.

The creek was swollen and noisy, hiccupping and muttering as it climbed higher up the bank. Bill jumped without slowing and again a surge of power spread through me.

Was the horse part of me or was I part of the horse?

At the top of the hill, Bill (or was it I?) stopped. The rain poured down, the clouds low, heavy and edged with light, tumbling over and over with threatening rumbles.

Gazing up, I had a sudden shift of focus. I was riding a wild, bucking surging world, on the edge of the tossing abyss of eternity.

A ragged edge of black cloud rolled in the sky, spreading the light of the moon. The rain turned silver and flooded over me. I shut my eyes and felt the silver go right through me washing the peace and belonging deeper in. There was the feel of warm rain on my face, warm horse beneath my legs and I blinked open my eyes.

It no longer mattered. I was me and I belonged. I wasn't sure where, but the confidence and trust were right through me. Bill knew. He turned and paced with steady steps down the hill, splashing through the creek back to his paddock.

I brought Bill to a halt at the gate. In a kind of trance I dismounted and opened it. Bill whickered a farewell and trotted off.

All the way home, up the long paddock, along the black lane, and across the black ribbon of road, the soft rain washed comfort and promise through me. I threw the bridle under the house and climbed back through the window.

The room was airless and stuffy, a confined prison smell, but that no longer worried me. I stuffed my wet clothes and runners as far under the bed as possible and climbed between the sheets.

In the morning, Mum would find them and start the usual complaints. It wasn't important anymore. It didn't irritate me to think about it.

I started to forget what promise was in the rain and black night, or the revelation that the silver of the moon had revealed. I had metamorphosed but I couldn't remember into what. I was thirteen years old, and at peace with my environment.

Chance Encounter

Janice Williams

While savouring the moon-glazed sea
I saw the child I used to be
The distant lights in sable skies
Reflected in her silver eyes
She capered lightly as a colt
And turned a graceful somersault
Then cartwheeled once, to barefoot land
And prance along the lustrous strand

The phosphorescence on the sea
She snatched, a sequinned shawl to be
A song she sang: 'My spell I'll share
Come dance as if there's no one there
You'll free your voice on silver wing
And find your 'what if?' words to sing
You'll laugh through diamond-spangled tears
And skip along the shore of years'

I shed my shoes, and ran to reach
My doppelganger on the beach
To dance in heart-step with this elf
This argent wisp, who was myself
But tossing iridescent hair
And splashing wavelets without care
My fairy disappeared from sight
And left me standing in the night

The Lesson

Sue Gunningham

I barely notice the footpath, trampled grey and dusty beneath a thousand hurrying feet. I count the sea of maroon-and-blue students ahead of me, then glare back at the stragglers. I wonder if they'll make it to the train station on time. These cosseted, overprotected children, unaccustomed to walking, ignorant of public transport timetables, expecting the train, like their parents, will wait for them, that everyone will have a seat.

I ignore the mumbles of "How much further do we have to walk?" and instead think back to my own childhood – raised in a house without a car, when prams were huge and carried baby, toddler and most of the groceries, while the elder two, like beasts of burden, trudged beside, laden with whatever we were told to carry from our weekly pilgrimage in search of food, and no use complaining that it's too heavy or I'm too tired or too little.

Today's kids are so different. They play 'make-believe' tennis on computer programs in their lounge room, and engage in unsocial conversations on social media, scribble on walls as a caricature of 'art' and savour reality TV that shows facsimiles of no-one's reality.

The herd on the footpath ahead swerves to the right and eddies around someone, sitting, dishevelled and dirty, pressed against a wall. His back to the wall, him against us, a cardboard sign that asks for help and although I 'gave at the office,' my skin crawls at the sight. I recollect reading somewhere that no-one in Victoria needs to be homeless, that it is their own choosing. I don't look at him, but skim over his head, nose up-turned, and he blends into the footpath and spares me his eye contact, instead concentrates on the well-shod and urgent feet, hurrying past to get from here to there, to somewhere else. The students huddle together and whisper 'homeless' into each others' squeaky clean ears.

Yet I hear it, hear "Miss, Miss!" behind me, and irritated I turn to see a lone straggler wrestling with his school bag, and I am conscious of the student herd ahead surging forward towards the train and home, and I sigh and my eyebrows question and he replies, "I'm going to give him something," and I think for drugs, for booze and why bother? The boy appears and disappears in the passing crowd and I worry he'll offer silver coins from his pocket money and be abused by the un-gentleman, sitting cross-legged. The fear of mental health issues sounds a warning in my head, but before I can move, the boy pushes through the press of moving flesh. I watch as he taps a filthy shoulder and an unshaven face turns. A grimy hand accepts a child's lunch, packed by mummy dearest for her special boy, no hint of fear from one or shame from the other. A lad of ten is told, "Thanks, mate". A smile passes between two worlds. I snap "Hurry up," but softly now, and tell the boy to follow quickly, catch up. I lower my eyes, more humbled than I ever thought possible.

Balloon Debate

The next four pieces are arguments to keep a particular style of poetry from being thrown out of a balloon that is adrift.

Iambic Pentameter

Mary Jones

I ambic Pentameter – that sounds daunting, doesn't it, but it's really quite simple. There are different words for different rhythmical beats within a line of poetry. 'Iambic' means the basic rhythm of breathing, or heartbeats, or old-fashioned railway journeys – di DUM di DUM di DUM. 'Pentameter' means there are five of them in a line of poetry – di dum di dum di dum di dum di dum.

They form the basis on which a lot of classic poetry is built. They're used by Chaucer, Milton, Marlowe and Shakespeare. Also John Donne, Wordsworth, Tennyson, Dylan Thomas and Gerard Manley Hopkins, Yeats and Larkin… The list goes on, and is very long, so if you're throwing iambic pentameter out of this balloon you're going to leave huge gaps in the entire history of poetry written in English.

(Not to mention most of Shakespeare's plays – including Ophelia – they're largely written in blank verse, which is iambic pentameter that doesn't rhyme.)

After classical formal poetry began to fall into disfavour, especially in America, a very young T.S. Eliot wrote a perfect iambic pentameter sonnet with a complex rhyme scheme, before he threw away the rule book altogether.

The point being that there has to BE a rule book, in order for it to be thrown away. One of my favourite Australian poets, Clive James, has said that it's only now towards the end of his life that he finally feels he's beginning to get the hang of poetry – and his later works have got more and more formal in structure. His latest book is almost entirely in – yes, you've guessed it – iambic pentameter!

In order to write in an iambic rhythm, a poet needs to develop a feel for the rhythm of individual words and where their stresses fall. I would argue that this understanding of the inbuilt shape and stress of a word is essential for all poetry, and one of the main things that distinguishes it from prose.

For a lot of people it doesn't come easily, and has to be built up by reading a lot of classic or formal poetry with an open ear. (Shakespeare is a very good place to start.) But like almost anything that needs hard work to achieve, it's well worth the effort.

It even helps you to appreciate some of the cadences in really good prose writing. If you have a tin ear for poetry, you often have a tin ear for prose as well. So if iambic pentameter gets tossed overboard from this balloon, a large part of the underlying framework of good literature goes with it. Don't let that happen!

Unrhymed Verse

Janice Williams

Unrhymed verse is *not* chopped-up prose. Well, it shouldn't be, but there's bad verse in all forms. So I'll go on to say that release from regular rules gives the poet permission to use full imagination without worrying that there is no rhyme for orange or discombobulation; to choose a strong, satisfying word, rather than a lesser one for form's sake. A child can write it: perhaps badly, but that's how we all start. And the childlike right brain is less likely to be daunted by the editorial left.

Unrhymed verse *has* rules, but they are flexible – not of the counted syllable or the matched vowel, but of the pause, the natural rhythm of speech – echoing the heart, the indrawn breath, the skipping step. It plays with alliteration, repetition and cadence. It takes a thought, dresses it in doll's clothes, or drops it back in the toy box.

It's quirky. It asserts, 'It's poetry if I say it's poetry.' It loves metaphor and delights in pictures. Take Carl Sandberg's 'The Fog':

The fog comes
on little cat feet.
It sits looking
over harbor and city
on silent haunches
and then moves on.

It's a master of disguise. It pretends to be prose, then has you wondering. You won't find John F Kennedy or Martin Luther King in poetry books, but what about:

I have a dream that my little children will one day live in a country where…' et cetera. It finishes: *'The rough places will be made plain, and the crooked places will be made straight. And the glory of the Lord shall be revealed, and all flesh shall see it together.'*

Note the loan from the Bible, famous for non-rhymed poetry, and use of picture, comparison and contrast.

Is *this* poetry?

> *Ask not what your country can do for you*
> *Ask what you can do for your country*

If: *'Yet strong in will / To strive, to seek, to find, and not to yield'*, is poetry, what about: *'We choose to go to the moon / and do the other things / not because they are easy / but because they are hard.'* (Could that be vers libre?)

The lines resound through decades. Isn't that what is expected of poetry? Unrhymed verse is a chameleon, constantly changing colour.

Consider Ophelia's mad speech in *Hamlet*.

> *There's rosemary, that's for remembrance. Pray you, love, remember. And there's pansies, that's for thoughts.*

Alliteration, image, repetition. In the same speech Shakespeare gives Ophelia:

> *They bore him barefaced on the bier, (hey non nonny)*
> *And in his grave rained many a tear.*

Which is more poignant?

Unrhymed verse is free to vary its pace. *The Man from Snowy River* is a well-loved poem; but it needs presentation like Leonard Teale's, or the hearer might fall off the horse with boredom.

Free verse forms stir feeling, make memory-associations, and lend themselves to performance. In *Les Miserables*, the revolutionaries are threatened:

> *You at the barricade listen to this:*
> *No one is coming to help you to fight*
> *You're on your own, you have no friends…*

Heavy cadence, clipped jackboot power of authority; the hearer knows that upholders of liberty, like poets, will not be quenched for ever. It brings to my mind the Chinese student in Tiananmen Square opposing a tank. I wonder if he wrote poetry.

The writer of unrhymed verse, like Thoreau's Man, does not always 'keep pace with his companions'. Perhaps he, too, hears a different drummer. 'Let him step to the music which he hears, however measured or far away.'

Should unrhymed verse be retained in the balloon? Certainly. It speaks with human vibrancy. But if it were thrown out, it would float gently to earth under the parachute of its own originality.

In Defence of Rhyme

Leigh Hay

As I'm offered five precious minutes of time
in a descending balloon, defending rhyme,
chances like this don't come every day
so I figured I might as well have my say
for rhyming verse is encoded in your DNA
bet you didn't know that before today!!

Rhyming verse begins at the cradle –
nursery rhymes and the occasional fable,
then simple rhyme progresses to school
with skipping ropes, rhyme's a chanting tool :
Cinderalla, dressed in yella, went upstairs to kiss her fella,
made a mistake, kissed a snake, how many doctors did it take?
One, two, three, four.….and so the ditty goes
while the skipping rope circles 'til it tangles your toes.

By senior primary we're into rhyming limericks
Knock Knock jokes and other assorted tricks
and if the teacher requests a poem, that's altogether fine
we simply create innate rhyme.
Because for little kids it's like the tick of a clock
the chime of a rhyme from Dahl to Belloc.
We seek rhyming words for bum, fart and loo
and we giggle our way through Winnie the Pooh.

From primary school on, we learn serious rhymes,
Wordsworth, Keats and Shakespeare's lines,
Our teachers tell us that rhyme gives meaning
structure, humour and romantic leaning
to poetry, tying words together in our mind

reinforcing similarities, related concepts of a kind.
Rhyming verse can showcase your wit,
you can play with rhyming words to make them all fit!

First, pick your word to express a thought or image
then Google your mind like shredding a cabbage.
Build on your words and let your poem flow
with traditional rhyming – hot to go.
Internal rhyme rhymes within the same line
in external rhyme the ends of two lines rhyme.
Half rhyme is when final consonants repeat
in Pararhyme consonants match, but vowels do a delete.

Cast your mind to the rhyming verse of Paterson and Lawson
or the advertising jingles of stuff to spend your money on.
Imagine if pop songs failed to rhyme,
like *Scarborough Fair's* Rosemary and Thyme?
We'd have no National Anthem without rhyming verse –
an omission I suspect to make Her Majesty terse.
And gift cards have to rhyme in a genre known as 'twee'
Sorry to hear your parrot died, extending sympathy and tea.

So if I haven't yet convinced you in the confines of this room
to wallow in the joy of rhyme and keep me in the balloon,
just think of all the poetry greats, of centuries gone before
Free Verse was ill considered, by those grand old poets of
yore –
They wrote with flourish and romance, a Highwayman riding
the moor
where the road was a ribbon of moonlight, up to the old inn
door.
Rhyme is food to the poetic soul and music to the receiver,
our favourite rhymes are n'ere forgot, but held close to our
hearts **forever!**

In Defence of Haiku

Janet Howie

Haiku ku … ku, the very sound of the name is charming, elegant and mysterious.

Haiku has a romantic history: It began in the Japanese Emperor's court where witty and intelligent people composed haiku spontaneously in collaboration to create a linked longer poem called renga. The first verse later became a haiku on its own.

A haiku is a very short poem. That's agreed. It can be traditional three lines, 5/7/5 syllables in Japanese language. Modern English haiku can be three lines, generally about 14 syllables, or two lines and even one line. Punctuation is minimal and mostly uses lower case.

Haiku:

- aims for the essence of things, compact but the meaning expands on reflection.
- uses spare, simple and apt language, involving the very rewarding search for the right word
- has seasonal and cultural references
- connects to special moments in nature and human experience.
- can be urban and experimental
- can be objective and subjective
- works in a variety of ways – riddle or puzzle, different angles on the familiar, emotion, humour and satire.
- uses juxtaposition. The first subject line, often ending in a dash or cut, is followed by surprising but related insights in line 2 and or 3, leading to further reflection.
- is used in haibun – a short recount of a journey or experience, with one to three haiku interspersed to provide a new but relevant angle. This form is based on the great Haiku master, Basho's journal, 'The Narrow Road to the Deep North'.

- also forms the first three lines of a tanka that adds on a couplet.
- becomes haiga when accompanied by a drawing or painting, the verbal and visual combining to make meaning richer.
- is practised and read world-wide in many languages.

Haiku came to the West after World War 2 and spread rapidly especially in Britain and America. The haiku of Basho, Buson, Issa and Shiki (the four Masters) became popular and people started writing and experimenting.

Haiku began in its traditional form, then after much debate and practice, evolved into modern English haiku. Everyone can have a go at writing haiku.

Haiku even came to Australia and our haiku poets have contributed well at home and on the international scene.

Haiku even came to me at a meeting of our Society of Women Writers, Victoria in 1998 when I was a new member. I was blown away.

Our speaker, Pat Kelsall, from Ballarat, spoke about Haiku and a new magazine called 'Yellow Moon' dedicated to understanding haiku and its related forms. I still have all the copies of Yellow Moon that was published until 2006.

Pat Kelsall wrote one of Basho's famous haikus on the white board and I've never forgotten it. There are a number of slightly varying translations:

on a bare branch
a crow has settled
autumn evening

This apparently simple haiku conveys the bleakness of the

autumn season. The crow has no shelter and the cold is coming down. The mood is sombre.

The magic and wisdom of haiku gripped me that day and my haiku journey began. It still goes on. I am open to haiku moments wherever I go.

The Society of Women Writers Victoria Inc A0039632B

The Society provides:

- Monthly meeting and newsletter *Write Away*
- Specialist speakers
- Biannual journal: *Sparx*
- Postal workshops
- Publication of occasional anthologies
- Book launches
- Competitions and awards
- Interstate network with like-minded writers
- Literary seminars.

> **President**
> Paula Wilson
> email: paulawilson1@optusnet.com.au

> **Membership secretary**
> Del Nightingale
> email: dnightingale233@gmail.com

To apply for membership
send the application form and cheque or money order to:

> The Membership Secretary SWWVic Inc
> C/- Ross House
> 247 Flinders Lane
> Melbourne VIC 3000

SWW Vic aims to draw together women engaged in diverse writing genres.

Meet monthly on the last Friday of each month (February–November inclusive)

Ross House, 247 Flinders Lane, Melbourne VIC 3000
OR

Library at the Dock, Victoria Harbour 10.00am–3.00pm

- Program includes workshops and/or guest speakers and critical readings
- Visitors and guests are welcome
- Tea/coffee available
- BYO lunch
- Entry fee $5

SWW Vic also offers

- Entry to competitions run by the society
- Possible inclusion in biannual anthology
- Workshops by correspondence: available to members isolated by geography/personal circumstance, designed for members who are unable to attend meetings but available to other members.

AWARDS
The opportunity to compete for biennial awards:

- The **Margaret Hazzard Perpetual Trophy** for a short story (open to members throughout Australia)
- The **Kathryn Purnell Award** for poetry (Victorian members only)
- **SWWV Biennial Literary Award** in various genres for women writers across Australia
- The **Nance Donkin Award** for a woman writer of books for children (inaugurated 2009)

https://www.facebook.com/societywomenwritersvic/

To find out more, visit the SWWV website:

www.swwvic.org.au

MEMBERSHIP APPLICATION

SWW Vic Inc A0039632B

Name ____

Address ____

_________________________________ Postcode _________

Phone (home) _______________________________________

Phone (business hours) _______________________________

Email ____

Writing Interests ____________________________________

____

____

Annual fee (1st July–30th June): $45.00 (including GST).

For those who join after 1st January, the fee is $25.00 for the remainder of the financial year. Please add $10.00 for the year if joining a Postal Workshop.

Send this form with payment to the Membership Secretary.

Annual membership is due and payable 30th June each year.

For queries, contact:

> **Membership secretary**
> Del Nightingale
> email: dnightingale233@gmail.com

To apply for membership
send the application form and cheque or money order to:

> **The Membership Secretary SWWVic Inc**
> C/- Ross House
> 247 Flinders Lane
> Melbourne VIC 3000